THE GUIN SAGA

Book One: The Leopard Mask

KAORU KURIMOTO

TRANSLATED BY ALEXANDER O. SMITH

WITH ELYE J. ALEXANDER

VERTICAL.

Published by Vertical, Inc., New York.

Originally published in Japanese as *Hyoto no Kamen* by Hayakawa Shobo, Tokyo, 1979.

ISBN 978-1-932234-81-7

Manufactured in the United States of America

First Paperback Edition

Vertical, Inc.
1185 Avenue of the Americas 32nd floor
New York, NY 10036
www.vertical-inc.com

It was Jarn the destiny-weaver that guided their actions, yet they could not see the threads of fate upon which they walked. They did not know.

—From the Book of Illon

CONTENTS

Chapter One

THE SPIRIT WOOD

—— *Prologue* ——

Freakish, it was.

To call it "peculiar" was to deny the sheer bizarreness of the thing. But there, "bizarre" too fell short.

"Freakish" was all one could say, though the word hardly described the shock, the terror of seeing it.

For a while now—which is to say for most of half a day—the thing had lain there on its side. It did not move, but lay crumpled, like a corpse stricken and discarded.

Yet it lived.

For, now and then, its four limbs that lay stretched out on the ground would shudder, well-developed muscles twitching as if in seizure.

But that was the only sign.

The place where it lay was covered in silence that seemed eternal; the stillness was near complete. Evening was close, and the sun had waxed to a gigantic disk that shone with a dull hard light as it dipped low toward the mountains.

Had any man come wandering here this evening and seen the thing lying there, with its head half in the waters of the spring, he would have known fear—fear that gripped him and would not let go, that made his legs go weak. Doubts would have raced through his mind. Perhaps he had broken some sacred taboo; perhaps by seeing this thing, he was overstepping the boundaries that protected the safe, sane world that he had taken for granted. But in truth, none of sound mind would come here in the deepening twilight, for these were the lands of Stafolos Keep. These were the borderlands between the domain of men and the darker regions where darker things ran wild.

As freakish as the fallen creature was, it had the shape of a man. Still, few would venture calling it such.

Except for a crude leather loincloth, it was naked, its powerful body exposed, sculpted by training, hardened by battle. That body shook again—unconsciously gripped by equal amounts of thirst and pain. Slowly, it reached out its hands, caked with residues of blood and scored with countless battle scars. Slowly, they stretched toward the spring water that gurgled from the ground and spread into a beckoning pool.

The creature's hands broke the surface of the spring, palms cupped to scoop out water and lift it, trembling, to the mouth. The thing—or perhaps it was a "he"—was terribly thirsty. So thirsty that, if he did not drink, he would surely die.

Yet drink he could not.

His hands brought the water to his mouth, and there it stopped. Two times he tried; the water reached his lips, but went no further. A third time he strained, and the water ran from his shuddering fingers, and slid down his chin, while thirst raged in his throat.

A noise escaped his lips then, like the howl of a wounded, dying animal. The chilling cry shook the pool and stirred the bushes at the edges of the spring where small creatures—probably the winged taulos, half bird, half beast—took to the air in fright.

He reached out his hands toward the water a final time, and his strength left him. The hands dropped to the ground. Convulsions shook his frame, and he collapsed. Soon he became as still as he had been before.

Wind blew, rustling the grass, sending ripples across the surface of the spring. A grass viper's shining crimson eyes peered inquisitively from the underbrush for a moment and then vanished. Above, vampire vines came snaking down from the tops of strangely hued, misshapen trees. Yet he—or maybe it was an "it" after all—lay still on the ground, unaware of these things.

There it lay, on the ground by the spring, sprawled out in all its freakishness, unmoving, and defenseless.

—— I ——

"Rinda?" a shrill voice called out. "Rinda!"

The boy had meant to whisper but his voice rang out clear and loud, echoing through the vast grim silence of the forest.

"Shh! Be quiet!" came a young girl's sharp reply from the foliage nearby. Remus stuck out his lower lip in a pout, but the unseen Rinda was far from finished with him.

"Really! Is that cotton you've got between your ears? Have you forgotten where we are?"

"But—" her brother began.

"The Roodwood!" her voice came again, cutting him off. "In the lands of the tyrant king of Gohra!"

"But Rinda," he continued, slowly craning his neck out of the bushes to look around, "I thought you'd gone and left me."

"It's all right anyway. I think those riders have left." Rinda's head slowly emerged from the bushes a short distance away. She checked to make sure the horsemen really had gone past them without her brother's unfortunate display catching their attention. Finding that all was quiet around them, she slowly began the difficult and painful process of extricating herself from the shrubbery.

The bushes were those of the vasya, known for its delectable fruit and for the uninviting thorns that bristled from its leaves and even from its fruit. Rinda took the utmost care in pushing them aside, stretching out her slender white arms to hold down the thorny stalks as she wormed her way out of her hiding place. First her shining platinum blonde hair, then her slender, bare shoulders, then her delicate undeveloped torso, and finally, her legs, long and slim like a boy's in tall leather boots, emerged from the thorny hiding place where they had spent most of a day and a night.

"Ah! There isn't a bit of me that isn't positively prickling with pain." She shook herself and began to stretch her cramped limbs, but a little cry from her brother interrupted her long-awaited exercise.

She ran over to find that he was having considerably more difficulty than she had in extracting himself from his uncomfortable nest. He was fighting a losing battle against the thorn-covered leaves and stalks that caught on the soft skin of his hands and legs, leaving cruel trails wherever they touched.

"Can you do nothing right? The way you're thrashing

about, you'd think you wanted to cover yourself with scratches."
Rinda showed no restraint in her criticism as she helped him to
his feet and deftly plucked out the vasya twigs tangled in the
boy's platinum blond hair.

Standing there, their hands joined, the two looked amaz-
ingly alike—which was not surprising, since they were twins.
There in the shadowy undergrowth of the forest, they shone
like two perfect pearls, with their matched leather jerkins and
leather boots, and their silver short swords hanging from their
belts. They had the same braided platinum blond hair, the
same beautiful face—Rinda's intent and spirited, her brother's
innocent and carefree—and the same mischievous violet eyes.
They were like two sylvan spirits; so beautiful, it was a shame no
one was there to see them.

The twins themselves, however, could not care less about
appearances at the moment. Indeed, they were perfectly happy
not to be seen.

Remus rubbed his hands and legs where the thorns had left
him with more scratches than skin. As soon as he was on his
feet, he began whining.

"Rinda, what do we do now? I'm starving!"

Rinda turned her attention to the gear at her waist. Next to
the short sword, a soft leather satchel hung on her thick leather
belt. But even after a careful scrutiny of its contents, she could

find nothing that seemed useful in their current situation.

"Well, I didn't think of bringing any traveling food. With everything that was going on, it's a miracle I brought anything at all."

"So let's hunt—perhaps we can catch something to eat."

"I think not," said Rinda. "We haven't come to the Roodwood for a summer picnic, Remus. How many times must I tell you? We can't be running about chasing after animals. You know what would happen should someone from Stafolos Keep discover us? Even if we did catch something, we wouldn't be able to light a fire to cook it. You're welcome to eat raw taulos innards if you wish, but I'll pass, thank you very much."

"But... I'm so hungry I could faint."

"You're not the only one, you—" Rinda seemed on the verge of another scathing critique, but she suddenly broke off and looked around. "Did you hear that?"

"Hear what?"

"Hoofbeats! The riders are coming back!" Rinda shushed her brother before he could protest and dived back into the vasya thicket, heedless now of the clinging thorns. Though any who beheld her would have seen the promise of a dazzlingly beautiful woman—a few years were all that she lacked—she was not yet of an age to worry about her beauty or about preserving the rare softness of her skin.

"Remus! Quick!" Rinda hissed at her brother, who was still standing, quizzically cupping a hand to one ear. He turned and made to crawl into the thicket—but too late. The overgrown track that passed through the forest hard by the thicket where the twins had been hiding was suddenly filled with the pounding hooves of a squad of black-garbed riders. Their leader, the black plume atop his black helm fluttering in the wind, barked a sharp order through his faceplate, and the riders drew up and leapt from their horses in unison. All wore the same black helms and black cloaks, with faceplates down and great broadswords slung across their backs.

"Remus, run!" Rinda screamed. Remus had given up trying to force his way back into the thicket and instead turned and dashed for the woods—but one of the riders, moving swiftly, grabbed his slender arm in a grip like a vise.

"Let me go!" Remus screamed and struggled. His small face shone with the kind of prideful rage that only the most noble of blood and heart can muster.

The rider with the black plume gave another sharp order. *"Get them"*—he said *"Get them,"* thought Rinda. The language he spoke was not foreign to the twins, but the accent was so thick that it took her a considerable amount of effort to decipher the meaning. Remus screamed even louder as the other riders approached the vasya thicket. Heedless of the thorny bower into which Rinda had wormed her way, a hand sheathed in a gauntlet of cold iron reached in to snatch her as she clawed and twisted like an angry kitten.

Her captor seemed oblivious to Rinda's screams at the thorns that caught on her skin and in her hair. He dragged her roughly from the thicket and she tumbled out onto the grass where she caught her breath in ragged gasps, tears welling in her eyes from the scratches covering her body and face.

"Barbarians! Beasts! Swine of Gohra!" Rinda's deep violet eyes blazed with anger. "Why are you doing this? You Gohran dogs have taken everything from us! May Janos' bolts strike you and turn you to ash!"

The black-cloaked riders looked down coldly at the girl whose slender body shook now as her tears of pain turned to tears of rage. The captain laughed harshly, then suddenly, stepped forward. With his iron-gloved hand he grabbed her chin and looked at her face. His intent was clear.

"Let her go!" Remus shouted and strained against his captors, but their hands held him fast. Recoiling, Rinda spat at the mask covering the leader's face, and then in one swift motion leapt deftly out of his grasp and drew the short sword from the sheath at her waist.

She crouched like a mountain cat, fierce and proud. But her sword—a finely ornamented thing wrought of silver—was too slender to seem a threat. The men guffawed and cheered her on as their captain gave a guttural laugh and strode boldly toward her.

Rinda raised her sword and drew back; the black rider closed in. She stepped back again, but this time her foot caught on a tangle of weeds. She yelped and fell backwards, and the black rider leapt atop her.

"Rinda!"

The girl heard her brother scream as strong hands pinned her down to the ground. She fought wildly, with all her heart, struggling to get free. But her strength and her will were nearly exhausted.

"Rinda!" Remus screamed again and squirmed, trying to wrench out of the rider's steel grip, and then—

And then everything stopped. There was a sudden silence so complete that Remus could hear the breath catch in his captor's throat. The captain rolled off of Rinda and froze. Beneath his faceplate his eyes were wide with disbelief and terror. Rinda cried out weakly, but that sound too vanished into the overwhelming silence that had swooped upon the glade.

Slowly, slowly, something had stepped from the shade of the trees and begun walking toward them. The way it walked, with both arms stretched out before it like a mindless zombie feeling its way along, spoke somehow of things more horrible than death. Its steps were unsteady; yet, as it approached, its gait became increasingly stable and determined.

"W-What may't be?!" spoke a rider unconsciously, his voice trembling.

"'Tis a Rood demon!"

"A walking corpse!"

"A monster!"

A wave of fear rippled through the men. It was as if a nightmare had crept out of the darkest corner of their superstitious minds and was now stalking quietly through the gloom of the trees. It was coming for them.

"Janos! Mercy!" One of the weak of heart shouted a prayer and bolted toward his horse. The sudden movement broke the spell holding the riders. They tossed Remus aside and made a mad dash for their steeds.

"Hold! Who gave orders to mount? Who!" the captain shouted in wild frustration. He was nearly dumb with fear, and his hands shook, but he was their leader, and he had not forgotten his duty.

Rinda moved swiftly. As soon as the grip on her arm relaxed she pulled away and dashed toward her brother.

"Wait!" the captain called out. He took a step to follow her, momentarily forgetting the freakish horror in his chagrin at letting the girl go.

"You! Get them! The twins of Parros must not—"

His voice broke off in mid-order. The fiend's out-stretched hand had yanked him backward by the black plume atop his helmet. Its two giant hands then closed upon his throat. He yelped and twisted to draw the sword at his waist—but it was barely halfway out of its scabbard when the man's neck broke with a wet popping sound. The leader's head was now hanging backward at an unnatural angle in the powerful hands of the thing.

"Captain!" The riders stopped in their tracks. Though fear had nearly robbed them of their wits, these were trained soldiers, not a band of cowering children. Seeing their leader fall broke the spell of fear. They turned from their horses, drew their swords, and moved to surround the creature.

A strange, menacing sound, like the howl of an animal, came from the creature's mouth. One of the riders leapt forward, his sword-blade slashing down. The creature lifted the captain's body and blocked the swinging blade—and battle was joined. At once the wood was filled with cries and shouts and the clanging of blades and armor.

The twins of Parros had been completely forgotten. Indeed, the twins themselves had forgotten to escape and instead stood frozen with fear, watching the strange struggle unfold before them. Side by side, they held hands, their bodies trembling uncontrollably. Just days before, they had witnessed a battle on a much greater scale—the hellish pandemonium that had led to their exile in this backwater province. Then, too, they had stood watching, holding hands as they did now; but even the defense of Parros, bitterly fought against the Gohran invaders, could not compare to the bizarre conflict going on here, deep in the Roodwood.

"Rinda!" Remus whispered, bewitched by the scene before him, his entire body shaking, making jumbles of his words. "What is...What could it be, that thing?"

"H-How should I know?!" Rinda's teeth chattered, and only with a great deal of effort was she able to croak out an answer at all. "I...I think it's the Evil One, Doal, himself!"

"O gods, help us!" The words spilled unbidden from the boy's lips. Before his eyes, the man-thing was dancing between the blades of ten seasoned swordsmen; it—he—moved with steps that seemed far too light for his great mass. And slowly, but surely, he was killing the men. The strange being's only weapons were his preternatural strength and the captain's body, which he swung in deadly arcs like a great armored bludgeon. Already, three of the riders had fallen, heads smashed by their own leader's corpse. Two more had broken arms.

"It is Doal! He is—he has the strength of a god!" said Rinda. Remus looked at his sister in surprise. She was entranced, almost in rapture, watching the macabre dance.

"Why doesn't he pick up one of their swords and use that instead of the captain? Why, Remus?" she exclaimed. Indeed, she seemed almost on the verge of running in to council him on his choice of weapons, when the creature spun the body around and threw it like a missile, knocking two of the riders flat. The remaining three looked around, and despaired.

One of the men, his ears ringing with the screams of his fellows and his feet sliding on the battle-slick ground, flew into a blind rage and hurled himself forward as best he could, sword raised toward his foe. The creature slipped past the blade and grabbed him, hugging him around the torso with arms as big as an average man's thighs. The rider screamed like one caught in the embrace of a great snake. His screams did not stop until his spine broke, armor and all. Then almost casually the man-thing relaxed his grip.

"Two left!" breathed Rinda.

"Get behind him!" yelled one of the two remaining soldiers, motioning for the other to circle around through the trees. But the creature, choosing his steps carefully, turned around while fending off the swordsman before him, and quickly moved to put a large tree at his back. Cursing, the first swordsman swung his sword back and then, using a tactic favored in Gohra, abruptly threw it like a spear. At just the moment when it seemed that the wide blade would pierce through the creature's bare arm, the man-thing spun aside and, in one smooth motion, knocked the sword from the air with the side of his hand, snatched it up from the ground, and charged.

It soon became obvious that the monster's seeming reluctance to pick up one of the fallen swords earlier was not due to any lack of skill with such weapons. He wielded the heavy blade easily, as if he had been raised with a sword in his hand. The Gohran rider before him had just turned to flee when his head flew from his neck, trailing a red arc through the air. Spinning around, the creature caught the last soldier fleeing for the deeper woods and split him from the back of the head to his shoulders.

"He did it!" shouted Rinda.

Remus tugged on her hand. "It...he...he's coming this way!"

Surely enough, the creature had turned where he stood among the trees. Still holding the blood-stained broadsword, he raised his unsettling gaze toward the twins. Aside from him, they were the only ones still standing and whole. Rinda had forgotten her fear and stood entranced, returning his gaze. Remus tugged again on her hand, but seeing the creature come closer yet, he bravely stepped forward and picked up a sword off the ground, and yelling brandished it.

"Rinda! Run!" But her brother's voice hardly reached

Rinda's ears. Drawn by the creature's incredible form, her eyes were fixed upon it; she could not tear them away. Her mind was under a siege of queries: *What was this creature? Was he human, or something more? What was this man-thing that had ripped apart a squad of fierce Gohran riders, a full eleven men, in the blink of an eye—and with his bare hands!*

Human or no, Rinda had no words to describe him. Surely, from his neck down he was human—though his physique was extraordinary. His was a body that would plunge even a champion of the great ring into embarrassment at his own inadequacy. Not only was it huge, but it was also perfectly trained, with muscles that held untold strength, suppleness, and agility. They were the creature's only armor, covering chest, shoulders, and arms. His wide shoulders and mighty torso, tapering down to a rippling abdomen, were a sight to behold; but Rinda noticed deeper, older scars from untreated wounds beneath the light scratches and the blood (most of it not the monster's own) from the fight just moments before, that marred an otherwise perfect form. Surely, he had fought countless times before, and against even greater numbers.

All this she could see because the creature wore nothing other than the hide wrapping that only just fit around his waist; even his feet were bare. Yet if she saw nothing else, she would have had to agree that this was a man.

It was what she saw from his neck up that forbade her.

Rinda's eyes opened wide, and she absentmindedly chewed at her knuckles, transfixed by the figure that had wandered out of some nightmare and that now stood before her. For atop this man's body was the head of a giant leopard. His mouth was turned up in a vicious snarl, revealing two enormous fangs, and his eyes were two fearsome blazes of burning yellow. And this leopard-headed man-beast, broadsword still hanging from his hand, was slowly walking toward the spot where Remus and Rinda stood motionless.

Just then, movement in the underbrush caught Rinda's eye. Behind the leopard-man, one of the riders that had been flattened underneath the captain's corpse had come to; gritting his teeth against the pain, he was now quietly cocking his arm behind him to throw his sword at the creature's broad back.

"Look out! Behind you!" shouted Rinda. Why she would aid this creature that was very likely—no, almost certainly— coming toward them with the darkest designs of delivering them to the fate of the black riders that lay scattered on the ground, she could not have said.

But before she knew it, she had shouted a warning—and the leopard-man's reaction was swift.

He spun around and knocked the blade from the air with a lightning-like parry, then closed the distance between himself and the rider with two great strides and drove his sword through his attacker's neck. His movements were precise and merciless, as though the spilling of blood was something to which he had become accustomed long ago.

Ah, Remus and I are surely next. Janos protect us! Rinda covered her mouth with her hands. Remus shook, still gripping the sword—yet just holding the heavy blade seemed to have taxed the strength of his slender arms to their limit.

Almost leisurely, the creature turned back around to face them. His two eyes shone with a ghoulish light, marking the two children where they stood. Then, to the twins' startlement, the broadsword dropped weakly from his hand. It seemed as though, all of a sudden, strength had left the leopard-man's entire body. All that force, all that vitality—and now he rocked side to side, and finally fell to his knees on the forest floor.

"What...What's wrong with him?" Remus's voice quaked. Rinda noticed the bestial face, and the hand, reaching out toward them as though he were asking something of them. The mouth moved as though he were going to speak, but all that leaked out was an unearthly, flattened sort of growl.

"He...he's asking for something. He wants us to do something," said Rinda.

"Rinda, let's go, now! The rider's horses! We can—"

"Remus!" Rinda's voice was half surprise, half outrage. "He's just saved our lives! Can't you see?"

"He? You mean to tell me that thing's human? Rinda—"

"Look!" said Rinda. The leopard-man's huge hands had gone to his throat. With his left hand, he grabbed his throat as though in pain, and he repeatedly scratched at his head with the right.

Rinda clapped her hands and shouted, "I understand!" as she rushed forward. Her brother dropped the heavy sword and tried to stop his sister, but she wouldn't so much as look back. "He's human, he's just had a leopard mask put on him! Look, he wants us to help him take it off!"

"Rinda! I don't think we should bother him—"said Remus, but his sister cut him off again.

"Well now! Have you lost your nerve as well as your sense of obligation?" Clearly, Rinda had made up her mind about what was going on. She strode forward without a bit of hesitation. "How can I help? What do you want me to do?"

She reached out a delicate hand to the leopard-man's blood-covered head, trying to see underneath the mask. The young girl with her slender, boyish figure, worrying over the great hulk of the leopard-man, looked like a rabbit or a frail little bird poised before a lion.

Then the leopard-man spoke. Or rather, the low whine he had been making slowly took the shape of words. "Guin... Guin."

Again and again, he spoke that word.

"What's that? Is that something you want? How can I help you?" Rinda repeated patiently. But just then, the great leopard-man's body lurched, and at last he fell on his side on the thick undergrowth of the forest. Rinda sprang aside as the great body slammed to the ground, but then, emboldened, came back and laid her hand on the man's shoulder, which was still sticky with blood.

Then she gave a start of surprise.

"Dear me, Remus! This man is sick! He seems very weakened. Why, to see him a few moments ago, who would have known? Remus...? Remus! Go to the spring and find something to bring some water in, quickly! If we don't do something now, I fear this man will die!"

"Um, Rinda, are you quite—" Remus began.

"If you stand there like a fool much longer, it'll be nightfall!" With all the air of one who is accustomed to being obeyed, Rinda pointed her unwilling brother into the woods toward the spring. Reluctantly, the boy stood up. His sister was completely taken with the man-creature—that was clear. She shook the last few brambles out of her glimmering hair, and, with a determined expression on her face, she sat down once again by the side of this man with the head of a leopard.

—— 2 ——

To greet the coming of night in the Marches requires a great deal of bravery.

This is true even should you have a roof over your head and four strong walls around you. As for camping outside, no man endowed with wits would ever consider it even in the direst of circumstances.

Growing up in the safety of the Middle Country, the hardships of the Marches were foreign to the twins of Parros—and the fiends, beasts, and barbarians that lived there mere fairy-tales. Fear had always been at a distance, never something that jumped out and bit into their hearts. Had it been otherwise, there was surely no way they would have spent an entire night in the Roodwood with the prickly vasya as their only shelter.

Even though Rinda and Remus were blissfully unaware of the good fortune that had protected them thus far, this was to be their second night in the forest, and if nothing else, the events of the day had taught them caution. The bodies of men—riders from Stafolos Keep—lay about them on the ground where they had fallen, and it was a certainty that more riders would be out searching for their missing brothers.

"Um, Rinda?" Remus spoke in a low, worried voice, their grim surroundings having a chilling effect on him.

"Not now! Go pick more of that grass!" Rinda spoke without even turning to look at him, so accustomed was she to her role as undisputed leader. She was busily tending to the wounded warrior that had saved them, washing his powerful arms and legs with a wetted cloth and applying a poultice of medicinal herbs.

"But the sun's going down!" her brother continued.

"I can see, you know."

"It'll be nightfall soon!"

"I know, that's precisely why I'm hurrying!"

"Let's build a fire then. I'll go get grass, okay?"

"No!" Rinda's voice was stern. "If they see the smoke from the keep, we're as good as caught!"

"But if we wait until dark—"

"Remus, I know why you're afraid." As she spoke, Rinda had propped up the man's leopard head and was now attempting to pour water through his lips, without much success. "It's because we're in the Marches, right? But what would you have us do? Shall we just sally over to Stafolos Keep and say, please sirs, we're afraid of the ghouls and demons in the woods, might we stay just one night? Think that would work?"

"But, but Rinda! Rinda..."

"My name is to be spoken, not whined," Rinda said, her eyes flashing. "Really, is that any way for the true heir to the throne of Parros to act?"

"But..."

"Strength, Remus. We have to live through this, somehow. Now, we've managed to get horses and swords, and there's food in the riders' saddlebags. If we can just make it through the night, tomorrow we can ride out to the road, maybe even find a town of some kind. But for tonight, we have no choice. We're staying here."

"We should have just left that thing you're taking care of alone and gotten away while it was still light."

"And lose our way in the accursed Roodwood and end up riding around in circles for all time? Don't be foolish! And besides, I always know the right path. After all..." Rinda furrowed her brow and spoke as though deep in thought, "after all I am a Seer of Parros."

Her brother fell silent. On the surface, the twins of Parros may have looked like two pearls from the same oyster, but Remus knew—had known for all of his fourteen years—that inside, they were different. For he lacked the power that should have been his by birthright along with the royal blood that flowed through his veins. He lacked the gift of foresight and clairvoyance, the gift of prophecy.

Rinda barely noticed her brother's injured silence. Instead, her face suddenly lit up, and she leaned over her giant patient.

"Remus, look! He's come awake!"

The leopard head shook from side to side, weakly at first and then with greater determination. The twilight was a pale lavender in the gloaming hour. Set in the leopard head, the man's eyes shone with an unearthly yellow glow in the deepening dusk. Then he turned to look at the two children leaning over him.

The giant maw moved slightly, and out came a low growl. Remus, startled, drew back, but Rinda stayed leaning close over him, holding his head in her delicate hands and trying to get across to him somehow that they were his friends.

"Water? You want water?"

When she lifted the Gohran helmet that her brother had used as a makeshift bucket to bring water from the spring, the leopard-man abruptly rose to a sitting position and reached out a hand, his eyes flashing.

But when he lifted the helm to his mouth, he growled

wildly in despair and frustration. The leopard mask placed on his head formed a barrier between face and water, preventing him from quenching his thirst.

Rinda tilted her head quizzically at his despair. Then suddenly, she clapped her hands together as an idea came to her. Standing up, she began to search around the clearing. After a while, she returned to her patient with a satisfied look on her face, brandishing her find—a single hollow stalk of straw. After demonstrating with the straw herself, she gave it to the man, who placed it between his lips and began, eagerly, to drink.

It was likely that a good nine-tenths of his weakened state was due to severe thirst and hunger. He seemed greatly improved after he had finished drinking—in what seemed to Rinda an impossibly brief period of time—the contents of the large helm.

"Who would do such a thing?" Rinda spoke as she gazed thoughtfully at the leopard head. "Why, if you put a mask like that on someone and left him alone, how would he eat or even drink? I tried to take it off while you were sleeping, you see, but it wouldn't budge. It's been fixed with some foul curse, I should imagine. But really, how could a powerful swordsman like you end up having something like that put on your head?"

The ears of the leopard head were bent forward attentively. From deep within the mask, two eyes sparkled with a penetrating light as they stared at Rinda, evidence he understood everything the girl said. The two gaps in the mask around his eyes were the only places where his true face showed through, but still, thought Rinda, so fierce was the suppressed rage and iron will hidden in those yellow eyes that she would not have been surprised to find that, in fact, they were the eyes of some wild creature and not a man's at all. When Rinda had finished speaking, the leopard-man raised his powerful hands and tried once again to pull off the mask.

His efforts were made in vain. He let his hands drop again and gave a low anguished growl, but he reached out again when Rinda offered him some of the dried meat rations she had taken from the black riders' saddlebags. It seemed the strips were easier to push through the mask than the water had been, and he soon began chewing on the dried meat hungrily.

"Well, at least you won't die of starvation, even if you can't get that off," proclaimed Rinda, seeming somewhat relaxed as she knelt to watch the ravenous man eat.

Remus stood nearby, staring in round-eyed wonder. "So, what, he's actually a human?" he asked with some doubt.

"More than you are sometimes, I should think!" said Rinda. "This leopard mask was put on him by some king or nobleman—or perhaps it was an evil sorcerer whose wrath he incurred. I'm sure of it! He certainly didn't put it on himself—

I can't imagine anyone who would! Yes, it must be the work of some sorcerer. Why else would it stick on like it does even when he struggles to remove it? We've saved you," she said, now turning to the leopard-headed warrior, "so we're your friends. Now, what can we call you?"

While Rinda had been talking, a change had come over the leopard-man. It seemed the food and water had succeeded in bringing him back to life, though doubtlessly his phenomenal strength and powers of recuperation had also helped. Still holding a strip of dried meat in his hand, he let out a muffled growl. Rinda jerked back, startled at first, until she realized that he was saying something, though the mask made his words hard to make out.

"What's that?" she prompted him again.

"Guin..."

"Guin?" asked Rinda. He seemed to be saying that one word over and over. "Is that your name?"

"I...I think so." Now his words were coming through more clearly.

"You can talk! I'm Rinda, and this is my twin brother, Remus. What land are you from? By the shade of your skin, I'd say you're not from the north, or are you?"

"Aurra..." was the only answer he gave.

"Pardon?" asked Rinda. "What was that?"

"Aurra…"

"Aurra? Is that where you're from?"

"I don't…know."

His words were horribly muffled and slow as he struggled to speak through the leopard-head mask. Rinda was starting to get irritated and clucked her tongue impatiently as she leaned toward him.

"Aurra…Guin…"

"So, tell me—how did you ever get this thing put on your head?"

"Um, Rinda?"

Remus might not have been as quick-witted and lively as his sister, nor was he a prophet, but he never lacked in practical sense and logic. While casting worried glances around at the deepening navy shades of dusk, he had seen that getting the leopard-man to speak enthralled his sister all the more every minute; she seemed to have forgotten their grim surroundings, where they were, and how much trouble they were in. Unable to restrain himself any longer, he reached out and grabbed Rinda's shoulder.

"What? That hurts!"

"Um, Rinda, the night…it's coming!"

"I know that!" Rinda snapped back, but her face had taken on a somewhat worried look. She took another look around to reassess their immediate situation, and finding the shadows of the approaching night far deeper than she had thought, she quickly made the sign of Janos.

"Excuse me," she said, turning back to the leopard-headed man. "The night's coming. The night is coming!"

"So it seems."

Whether the twins had become used to the speech of this man who called himself "Guin," or whether the water he had been drinking had finally soothed his parched throat, his words were much clearer now. He looked around them, deep into the viscous violet gloom that filled the woods and hid lurid promises of fear and horrors unknown.

The underbrush in the woods around them rippled and rustled as a billow of wind picked up, carrying with it a foul rotten odor. Vampire vines swished in the treetops, and the beady eyes of vipers and things far worse glimmered crimson in the thick brush below. Silent during the day, the forest was coming alive again, showing its true face in the dark of night.

"Is that a problem?" asked Guin.

Rinda clucked her tongue in despair and disbelief. "Really! Have you no idea where this is? This isn't the middle country anymore. Why, Stafolos Keep stands right on the border between the middle country and the Marches! Gohran rule is just a rumor in the wind out here, and even the black riders of

Mongaul wouldn't think of going farther than the Roodwood with anything less than a full company! And that's exactly why we've come to the forest to hide. Better demons that don't know where we are than riders that do, right?

"But not now, with night almost here!" she continued. "That might not be a bad thing where you're from, but here in the Marches, the night belongs to spirits and wildlings and worse! Night is when the forest dwellers come out!"

"That's why I want to make a fire," said Remus, hugging himself tightly, his teeth quietly chattering.

"No," said Rinda, reflexively turning him down. Then, after some thought, she gave in. "But I guess there's no way around it. The vasya bushes were enough to keep us safe for one night, but you're too big to hide there. Or wait, Guin, do you have some spirit blood in you? Are you not afraid of the night?"

For some reason, Rinda had been reluctant to call him by his name, and when the word left her mouth a peculiar, almost otherworldly shudder ran through her limbs. *What's wrong with me?*

Though well-versed in omens and signs of all kinds, suddenly Rinda was scared to examine with her inner eye the tremors that now shook her body. Aware of her brother's suspicious gaze, she followed his lead and wrapped her arms around herself and grabbed her shoulders, pretending that her shivering was due to the cold of the forest air.

The leopard-man, for his part, hadn't seemed to notice Rinda's discomfort at all. Instead, he had stretched his giant hands before his face and seemed to be engrossed in staring at them.

"I was wounded," he muttered so low that only Rinda could clearly hear him. "Here, too, a scar from a blade. I must have been in battle. But this—this looks not unlike the mark of a lash. The Marches? Stafolos Keep? This 'Roodwood,' I have heard of…but why would I have come here? An enigma, along with this—" Here he lifted his hand to finger the leopard mask where his head and face should have been. "How have I come to have this…this…"

"You mean you don't know?" shouted Rinda, putting her hands to her mouth in surprise. "You don't remember at all?"

"It…seems that way."

Thanks perhaps to the empathic abilities that ran in their blood, Rinda and Remus—particularly Rinda—had no trouble understanding Guin's speech after a while. Had it not been them, had he spoken to unattentive ears, the slow muffled speech emitted by the great leopard mouth would have sounded nothing so much like animal whines and growling.

"Whom did I fight?"

"Whom did you fight? Why, you demolished an entire squad of the Gohran duke's black riders!"

Rinda pointed at his handiwork as she spoke. The leopard-man looked around and shook his head in bewilderment.

"I did that?"

"And what's more, you saved us!"

"Rinda, can we make a fire? Please?" said Remus, almost shouting in his desperation, forcing Rinda back to the reality of their present situation.

"Right...right, of course. But you do know we're not going to make it through the night alive."

"Ghouls like the smell of blood, I hear," added Remus. It was a little bit of trivia he had learned a long time ago. "It can't be safe to be near these bodies."

"The spring!" said Rinda after some thought. "We'll just build a fire near the spring and spend the night between the water and the fire. The nixies won't come out of the water to bother us, and isn't fire the shield that Janos gave mankind? Right, and we'll have to take three horses with us, too. We'll need them, to ride out of this accursed forest at the first light of day."

"Why are..." began Guin, struggling to find the right words. "Why are you here, in a place of such danger?"

"Well, we were—" Remus began to reply when his sister gave

him a sharp pinch on the arm.

"The archduke of the Mongauli is after us," was all Rinda said. "Well, we'd better get going."

"Who am I?"

The giant man's voice was so soft it barely passed his lips, yet it was so full of raw anguish that Rinda, who had just now been in a great hurry, stopped and turned around.

"Who am I? 'Guin'—is that my name? With whom did I fight, and why am I in these woods? And this! For what possible reason could this have been put on me? What sorcery holds it, that it will not come off no matter what I do? As I sit here I cannot even recall my face.

"Was I being pursued," the leopard-man asked no one in particular, "or had I escaped from some punishment for a crime? Where was I born? Who taught me the way of the sword? I don't even know what kind of life I have lived; I remember nothing.

"And 'Aurra'...Like 'Guin'—the word that seems to be my name—this word 'Aurra' has been ringing in my head since I awoke. Aurra...Aurra? Is it some thing, or some person? What could it mean?

"My harbor, my house—my armor, my lord—where are these things? Is there a place where I might find peaceful sleep in the arms of a friend, or a place, where if I went, I would be hunted down, a wanted man, my life at risk? I...I do not know."

With this, the warrior grabbed the leopard head in his giant fists and strained, as though he had gone mad, to take it off. But the mask stayed stubbornly affixed to his head. Crouching down, he covered his head with his arms.

Seeing him troubled so, Rinda's kind heart was filled with sympathy. She placed a hand on the warrior's shoulder and tried to comfort him as though he were a child. "You must be quite tired, and you've been wounded in battle," she said, speaking gently in her sweetest voice. "I'm sure you'll remember everything in due time, and find out how to get rid of that mask, too. I'll do whatever I can to help.

"But for now, we must go. We are not welcome here. All will be better in the morning..."

3

It was a strange, bewitching night, not one the twins would soon forget.

Long afterwards the memory of it would come to them—to Rinda as she swam in the waters near Corsea or sat in a Mongauli tower, to Remus as he lay between sheets of Parros silk. Perhaps even the warrior Guin recalled it somewhere in the depths of his heart. It was a night as mysterious as the holy night of birth. There they were, where not even the hardened mercenaries of the Marches patrol would think of staying after sundown, deep in the borderland woods with only their blazing campfire between them and the ghosts, ghouls, and demons that roamed the night.

Not that the three sitting around the fire seemed entirely out of place. The twins could easily have passed for naiades or dryads had they been wearing light white robes instead of their battered travel garb—so like spirits they were, with their frost-colored hair sparkling in the firelight, violet eyes that looked almost silver in the darkness, and long, slender arms and legs. Their companion seemed to have come from another world entirely—a warrior of heroic proportions with a dark rage burning in the eyes that peered out from his ferocious-looking leopard mask.

At Rinda's suggestion, Guin had taken a black breastplate, iron gauntlets, and greaves from the corpse of the largest of the Gohran riders he had slain. He added to this a pair of high leather boots, strapped on the finest broadsword he could find, and hung a light but sturdy black cloak from his shoulders.

He did not take a helmet. Wearing one of the black helms of Gohra could have fatal consequences should they happen to encounter any of the barbarians or soldiers from one of the many lands that were at war with Gohra. Moreover, there was another, simpler reason—it was unlikely that any of the helms there would have fit over his giant features.

Rinda admitted to herself that, recovered from his exhaustion and with a full set of clothes, Guin cut quite a handsome figure. Even his strange leopard head seemed much less a horrifyingly wild thing. He was like a god, she thought—half-man, half-beast—a noble warrior infused with untold strength and an animal soul.

The three companions constantly supplied their bonfire

with oily grasses and branches to maintain its strength. The steadily burning flames cast their orange light in an alluring pool of wavering radiance that made for quite a fantastic sight. The circle of firelight carved out a small but certain territory; inside was the travelers' refuge, outside were the spirits and fiends to whom the black night of the Marches belonged.

The twins of Parros spread cloaks on the grass and sat themselves down. With their hands on their knees they huddled close together. Occasionally, they would shoot glances at the hostile darkness beyond the firelight's reach; then they would turn their gaze toward their mysterious companion who sat hunched over, the firelight glinting on his giant frame. Reflected sparks from the fire danced like little devils across the metal fittings of his armor, emphasizing his strange features. He was the stuff of warriors' nightmares.

In the darkness beyond, the shadows of things even darker writhed in vexation at the bold challenge of the campfire, outraged at this incursion into their territory. Even in the Marches, there was a clear borderline between the human and spirit worlds, and as long as people sat awake around a fire and it was clear that the rule of man was being upheld there, the spirits could not touch them. The Roodwood, a silent wilderness during the day, now teemed with unholy life, a swarm of ghostly things that did not walk the earth as men do; yet the flimsy boundary the three intruders had made with their circle of firelight kept them from harm.

But outside the hopelessly short range of the firelight, the forest-dwellers waited for a chance to do mischief. Rinda could hear the slithering sound of some giant thing sliding moistly through the underbrush, breathing in a ragged *syuu-syukk, syuu-syukk*. She could see the glinting eyes of shadowy things—several of them had gathered in the shallow darkness just beyond the reach of the light, making eerie noises that seemed to swish right past her ears. Once she heard the whoosh of giant wings as something took off, followed by the clamor of a desperate struggle; in the following quiet the horrifying snap-snap sound of bones crunching and the slurp of something drinking; then a flurry of commotion as the unseen predators quarreled over their prey.

Each time they heard a new noise, Rinda and Remus would huddle even closer and hold each other's hands more tightly. For fifteen years they had lived as an inseparable pair—so inseparable that, if they were ever separated, each would feel incomplete, like the lost half of a broken whole. But when they were together, no matter what happened, they could always find the strength to make it through. Still, this was too cruel a place for the twins—mere children, neither of them having performed the rites—to spend a night.

Rinda could hardly bear to sit silently any longer, listening to the freakish, fearful noises in the night. "It...it's really dark here, isn't it? I mean, the fire's not going out, right?" No sooner had the words left her mouth than she turned to Remus with a startled look on her face—

...the fire's not going out, right?

...going out, right?

...right?

...right?

The mocking sound of tree spirits echoing back her words filled the deep woods around them. The warrior Guin stiffened and sat upright. He didn't like the undisguised malice he could hear in their voices, and he put his hand on the grip of his broadsword.

"Don't worry, they're just mocker imps. They can't do anything to us," said Rinda, glaring out into the darkness, then turning back to the fire as if to ignore them. She changed the subject. "No sleeping, Remus! If you nod off for even a second you'll have nightmares, you know. Just pinch your knee if you start getting sleepy."

"I'm fine."

"You're far from it! This will be the second night we haven't slept, and it's going to be tough, but I know if we can just make it through until tomorrow..."

"Well you *don't* know that, do you, Rinda Farseer? Nobody knows whether we're going to see tomorrow or not," her brother replied, sulking. Rinda fell silent and briefly considered not saying anything back to her brother, until she remembered the dark sounds that crawled in the silence, and decided she much preferred her brother's complaints and the mockers.

"Tomorrow will come," she said, proudly lifting her silver head. "I know it. Tomorrow will come, and everything will be better. I mean, no matter how bad it is, it has to be better than yesterday, when we had to spend the night in the vasya bushes where it hurt just to breathe. Or the day before, galloping along, hanging on to those saddles for dear life and crying and crying. Or the day before that—" Rinda bit her tongue and fell silent as a horrible scene from her memory floated before her eyes. She quickly put her hands to her mouth.

"Rinda..."

"It's okay. I'm okay," she said. "We'll make it through this." But the look she gave her brother was filled with worry.

"You two..." said the leopard-headed warrior. It seemed he was at last taking genuine interest in what was going on around him. "Why are you two wandering in this wood? What brought you to this place?"

"Well, we were—"

"Quiet, Remus!" Rinda cut off her brother before turning to Guin. "Don't you know who your friends are? You saved us, and we saved you, but still you don't know?"

"I am no man's friend."

"That's what I'm talking about."

Rinda shivered slightly. The fire was still burning brightly; she shivered not because of the forest cold, but rather because she had felt something, the shadow of some giant creature that stirred the darkness with its passing.

"It's so very dark here," Rinda moaned. "And—can't you hear that sound over there? That's something gnawing on bones! It's creepy!"

"Rinda's a prophet—a seer," Remus explained to the warrior, sounding a little proud. "She's closer to the spirit world than me or other ordinary people. When we were born, the prophets of Parros foresaw that we would be two pearls—one an elixir, the other a treasure."

Guin was silent.

"They told me it meant Rinda would be a great prophet and a sorceress, and I the sovereign of Parros."

"Remus!" his sister said sharply, but Guin seemed to take an interest in what Remus was saying.

"Parros? Sovereign?"

"Yes, Parros! Even if you lost *most* of your memory, surely you still remember the Kingdom of Parros, pearl of the Middle Country?"

"The Kingdom...of Parros?"

"Yes, the Kingdom of Parros, ruled by His Holiness, Aldross the Third. But..." Rinda paused. "It is no more," she said flatly, realizing it was foolish to speak evasively any longer. Both twins' eyes welled with tears they had long held back; in their memory the image of the beautiful crystal spires of home blurred and ran, and once again they could see the horrible things they had been trying so hard to forget: towers burning and crumbling in the fires of war, people being cut down in the streets, everything falling, falling. "They torched the crystal tower, murdered the holy royal family, the king and the queen—who were granted their thrones by Janos Himself!—and all the crusaders of Parros, killed..." Rinda spoke softly, cursing the Gohrans. "I will not forget the blood that flowed under the blue moon, in the dragon year, not until the day I die."

"Did I fight in that battle?" asked Guin, more concerned about his forgotten identity than her loss.

"I wouldn't know," said Rinda brusquely, "but there's certainly no custom of putting leopard heads on prisoners in Parros, and I would think that someone trying to hide his face by putting on something like that would just end up attracting more attention. Now the Mongauli army of General Vlad, one

of the archdukes of Gohra, is known to do all sorts of despica-
ble things. But I've never heard of even them torturing or
restraining a person in such an odd fashion."

Rinda clicked her tongue, almost seeming upset that the act
of entrapping someone in a leopard mask couldn't be added to
the list of the Archduke of Mongaul's crimes.

"You know, I think this guy came from the Southlands,"
said Remus.

Rinda thought for a moment. "Well, that might be the case
and then again it might not," she declared, as if to put the issue
to rest for the moment. She was scanning the darkness around
them, her nervousness growing. "When the bards would sing of
spending a night in the Marches, gathered around a campfire,
it used to sound so nice, so romantic. I don't think I shall ever
want to hear one of those phonies playing the kitara and
chortling such nonsense again."

"I believe," said Guin, his voice rising abruptly as he looked
into the sky, "that we are on the verge of a much greater adventure than merely warming ourselves around a campfire."
Around them in the darkness, things swished and scattered,
startled by his sudden growling cry.

"What is it?"

"The wind is wet, and I smell rain. If a storm comes, our
fire is done for."

"How…" Rinda was at a loss. How could this warrior feel something that not even she, Rinda Farseer, could? The night air seemed no wetter than usual to her—unless he really did have the senses of a leopard?

But Rinda didn't wonder long. She knew that, if a real storm was coming, they were in a great deal of trouble—and soon she too could smell the wetness blowing in the wind. She bit her lip and shivered as a premonition wracked her body. The fire danced and trembled in the rising wind; beyond it, Rinda could sense the things that lived in the darkness moving back and forth, flapping and fluttering as they went.

"Jarn the weaver of fate is a spiteful old fool!" the girl exclaimed, punching her little fist up at the sky as she cursed. "He could have just let us sleep, but no—he won't even allow us to make it through one measly night, huddled around this fire. He must want very much to end our royal bloodline, that's what I think."

"Rinda, he's got a hundred ears! He'll hear you!" whispered Remus, hurriedly uttering a prayer of penance.

"I wouldn't care if each of those hundred ears were as long as a torris hare's, I really wouldn't!" said Rinda, a note of challenge in her voice. But she bit her lip and fell silent when she saw the clouds hastening ominously across the sky, and the trees lurching back and forth as though in spasms of agony, and the countless crimson eyes all turning to look in her direction, watching and waiting.

The twins held tight to each other's hands, wondering how they were going to get through this latest in a long series of calamities. The warrior Guin sat still with his shoulders hunched, glaring at the fire. He seemed either utterly unaware of, or utterly indifferent to, the approaching danger, so it surprised Remus and Rinda when he suddenly stood up and slapped the hilt of his broadsword.

"Careful! You'll make the fire go—" began Rinda, but the look in Guin's eyes made her break off. The warrior's eyes were gleaming in the firelight, but it was a gleaming filled with darkness—so much like the eyes watching the three from beyond their circle of firelight that, for a second, Rinda thought he was one of those things come into the light to kill them.

"Run with me, girl child! Follow close if you want to live to see daybreak!" Guin's voice was a howl. Quickly he swept down and picked up the longest stick from their pile, and after lighting it in the fire, thrust it upwards like a torch and ran off into the woods.

"Wait!"

In a flash, the twins shot to their feet and chased after the leopard-headed warrior, still holding hands. Guin was fast, but they managed to keep up with him.

An unseen force seemed to be guiding the leopard warrior, or perhaps it was the wildsense of a forest beast. Deftly, he dodged this way and that through trees that stood on all sides like eerie black skeletons, picking up a trail that had been lost for hundreds of years.

"Guin! Guin, please! Where are we going?" Remus called out, gasping for breath.

"Quiet! Save your strength!" Guin shouted back—then added quickly, "Stafolos Keep!"

"Rinda! Did you—" Remus began, but Rinda interrupted with a scream as a grass snake cut across their path. She quickly regained her composure, however, sensing that if she did not, she would surely perish.

"He's right!" she gasped as they ran. "Either we take over the keep, or wander through these woods until we die! I bet he can do it, too!"

"I said no talking! If you would live, run! To Stafolos Keep!" shouted Guin.

"Guin!" Rinda yelled. "Guin, listen! The horses! The horses, Guin!"

"What?"

"That clearing where you fought the Gohran riders! If their mounts are still there—"

"Right!"

Guin glanced quickly to both sides, then abruptly shot off in a new direction, guided by the instinct of a beast.

"If some fiend hasn't eaten those horses, we might just make it to Stafolos Keep before the storm!" Rinda panted, trying to ignore the pain in her legs, which were threatening to cramp any moment now. She was breathing hard, but every time it seemed like the torch in Guin's hand was pulling farther away, she thought she could feel the breath of some strange and horrible thing on her neck, raising goose bumps on her skin, and she would run harder. Remus caught her by the hand and tried to drag her along, but that just ended up slowing both of them down.

It was no good. Rinda stumbled and emitted a quick yelp as she fell to the ground—when suddenly she felt herself being lifted lightly into the air.

"Guin! No! Put me down!"

"Hold the torch steady! Unless you want to be eaten," Guin howled in reply. "If the vampire vines come down, use the torch on them—just don't let it go out!"

And the leopard-man ran weaving through the trees toward the clearing.

It was as though the darkness had bared its fangs at them. Whichever way they turned, countless crimson eyes glinted from the deep pools of shadow under the trees, and the night air was stirring, filled with the pulsing life of things that were not alive. The clouds drifting across the sky moved faster, and the companions' last, unreliable ally, the moon, vanished, the bluish-white light of the goddess Aeris simply blotted from the sky.

"Girl child!" howled Guin, stopping abruptly. "This is the place? You are sure?"

"I...I think so, but then..."

"Lift up the torch!"

Rinda was used to ordering people around and having her orders followed. To be issued an order, and in such a brusque manner—that was new to her. But there was something in the leopard-headed warrior's voice that made her listen, whether or not she wished to, and so Rinda did as she was told. Steeling herself, cringing in anticipation of a sight of strewn bodies and carnage everywhere, she thrust the torch out toward the clearing.

Remus gave a quiet gasp of surprise from where he stood clinging to Guin.

"They're gone! All gone!"

In the wavering light that spilled from their torch into the clearing, they could see the two vasya bushes with branches broken here and there where the riders had ripped them apart looking for their quarry. Beside them on the ground were the black helmets, a broken broadsword, and blood stains from the battle before. This was certainly the clearing where the riders had chased down the twins, where Guin had saved them.

But where the corpses of the fallen riders should have been, there was nothing. The man that Guin had crushed with his hands, the man he had beheaded with a single swing of his broadsword—all were gone. There were no horses tied between the trees, either, poking their noses into the grass or scratching the ground with their hooves in worried impatience.

"Guin?" said Rinda in a dry whisper.

"They were eaten," said the warrior, his voice a solemn growl.

"But Guin, what could—"

"Ghouls, wolves, giant adders, maybe something else."

"Oh!"

Rinda shut her eyes, and with her free hand, she grabbed onto Guin's leopard pelt as hard as she could. She felt as though some horror might emerge from the darkness any moment; but at the same time, she was starting to feel that, here with her arm around Guin's neck and her cheek pressed to the soft fur of his mane, they would be safe no matter what came.

Guin, standing with the girl perched lightly on his shoulder, assessed their situation in the blink of an eye. They had lost the horses, and it was still a formidable journey to Stafolos Keep. The distance wasn't actually too great, but he wouldn't have bet on their chances of reaching the fortress before the storm hit, and no warrior, no matter how courageous, wanted to weather a storm in the Marches. Even in the Marches, there were rules that governed the ways of spirits and men, that laid down a clear line separating them. The storm would suspend those rules.

The winds began to howl and rage, and the trees groaned and creaked. Then the three heard a fearful sound, like a woman's wail, trailing off into the distance—a sobbing shaitan, or a mountain wolf.

"Guin…" Remus's voice quavered. "There's something—"

"I know. They are come."

The darkness grew thicker, slowly drawing in around them. It was a wet, unpleasant mixture of murk and shadow and the only thing holding it at bay was the pitifully dim light of their torch, which now only barely succeeded at carving out a small patch of light from the darkness.

"Boy child," said Guin in a low growl, "get behind me, hold on to the belt beneath my cloak and move as I do. Girl child, hold tight onto my neck. I am of flesh and blood; I am a living man. As long as I fight, they will not harm you."

"But if the storm comes—"

"Then we shall beg for Jarn's pity."

Rinda, shaking, gripped the leopard mane as tightly as she could. While she had no idea what kind of past this man had buried in the valley of his lost memory, he seemed experienced in the world, and he had managed to survive thus far while wandering alone and wounded in the Marches. That experience, and his sword, were all the twins of Parros had to rely on now.

The wind began to howl even louder. In the darkness, the three could feel the things hiding between the trees surrounding them, hateful eyes watching for any sign of weakness.

Then suddenly something approached with terrible swiftness, and Rinda screamed.

Sliding from the darkness, flying directly toward them, was a thing with no arms, no legs, not even a body! It was a flying head, a hateful ghoul, swift, cold, and as pallid as chalk. Its bared fangs gnashed, lusting for warm blood and living flesh, and the ghastly spheres of its eyes reflected nothing as they roved. It flew through the air, trailing its spinal cord like a long stringy tail, lunged at the warrior and sought to sink its teeth into Rinda.

"Ahh!" Rinda slipped down Guin's shoulder. Guin hunched over to settle her firmly on his back, then grabbed the torch with his free hand and swung it at the ghoul.

The thing screeched out a deranged laugh and the air filled with the vile smell of dead flesh burning. Its scorched eye oozing pus, the flying head sailed away, mocking them with its laughter as it disappeared into the darkness.

"A ghoul," said Guin, switching the torch to his left hand and drawing his broadsword.

"But that was just a head!"

"Taken from one of the riders no doubt. They normally don't attack the living, but this one has grown bold. It must have feasted on the horses," Guin explained calmly—then all at once he was shouting. "It comes again!"

The ghoul had returned. The light of the torch shone on its clacking teeth and glistened off the charred skin on the side of its face. And then, they could see beyond it—

"Fiends!" shouted Guin, half cursing, half in warning. Out of the darkness behind the flying head came one, then two, then a dozen horrible things that once had been men. The riders had returned.

It was a macabre procession. One walked without a head. Another was split into two equal halves from neck to waist, the blood long since spilled onto the forest floor. A severed arm walked on lifeless fingers, following after a body that a great blunt weapon had beaten into a cruel caricature of the human form. The terrible spirit-denizen of the woods had animated these eerily familiar figures, the very black riders of Gohra that Guin had fought. Stalking among them was the hulking shape of their captain, his head grotesquely twisted around to look backwards for all eternity, white bone showing where his throat should have been. Behind him came the horses, naught left but their skeletons, drifting along like pale white shadows.

Between the storm-bent trees they came, creatures spawned of hell, writhing pale harbingers of misfortune. All were incomplete in some way, lacking eyes to see, or ears to hear—none could have had the full complement of five senses. Yet they needed them not: other forces guided them. They stirred in utter silence, and from them came rippling waves of a hideous craving, an eternal starvation that ate away at their accursed bodies, a hunger that would not be sated no matter how much dead flesh they consumed. Their cold burning desire was so strong it was tangible. Driven by an insatiable appetite, they attacked.

Guin let loose a beastly howl, and the air around him shook with the force of it. Swinging the great sword, he cut down ghouls left and right, the well-honed blade splitting heads in half, freeing twisted necks from torsos, slashing through the skeletal horses as if cutting through butter; all the while he spun agilely to protect the flaming torch in his left hand. That torch was their last hope for survival and their enemies knew that all too well. Many of the ghouls were purposely seeking to dart past the blade to get at it. And so Guin danced, cutting down the creatures every time he turned. For their part, they kept shuffling forward with no regard for self-preservation, making

his task a relatively easy one, though no more pleasant for that.

But then—

"Arragh!" Guin roared. "Accursed corpse eaters!" There was a reason the ghouls made no efforts to protect themselves—for each time his sword cut through a neck or sliced a torso sideways in half, the pieces would drop to the ground and draw back a short distance, oozing viscous goop but showing no other sign of discomfort. Then they would turn and attack again, now two or three ghastly assailants where once there had been only one.

"Guin!" Rinda screamed in fear, holding on to the warrior for dear life as he dodged back and forth. A severed arm had come looping crazily through the air and, avoiding both torch and sword, had latched on to Rinda's exposed shoulder. With a cry of disgust, she tried to pry off the cold fingers, but the arm clung fast to her warm skin like some horrible leech.

"Get off me! Get off!"

Hearing Rinda's screams, Guin switched the broadsword and torch to opposite hands in one swift motion, using his right hand to thrust the torch at the arm grabbing the girl. There was the horrible sound of flesh burning and blistering, and a moment later the arm dropped off its prey and fell into the bushes below. Rinda's arm was swollen and red where the thing had latched on, as if it had been trying to suck the life from her.

"Children!" Guin yelled to the twins as he continued slash-ing away ineffectively at the ever-advancing creatures. "Children, you must fight! I will count to three! Then I shall grab those branches there—you will take them and use them as torches! If you want to see the dawn, don't let the fire die!"

"All right, Guin!"

"Ready? One—two—three!"

On the count of three, Guin threw the torch into the air, then quickly bent and snatched up the branches. Immediately a disembodied head dripping foul humors and a blistered burnt torso closed in; but the leopard warrior, standing again, caught the precious flame before they could steal it. With the torch and branches safely in his left hand, Guin flicked the two fiends away with the sword in his right.

"Now! Light them!" he shouted, holding up the sticks. Rinda took them and lit them with the original torch, making two new torches.

"Remus—here!"

"Got it!"

Now there were three torches blazing brightly, forcing back the darkness. Yet the ghouls around them, driven by a demonic thirst, showed no sign of retreating. Grabbing tightly onto the warrior's belt, Remus joined the fight, swinging his torch at the rotting corpse-fragments advancing upon them.

"Guin..." On Guin's back, Rinda was holding up her new torch, but didn't dare swing it. Her voice was shaky and full of fear.

"What?"

"A drop of rain—on my cheek."

The storm was coming.

All around them, the ghouls were shuffling more quickly, a dark, gloomy kind of joy in their movements. They could hear the mocking laughter of coyotes in the distance, but the ghouls said nothing—their mouths gaping silently—though the expectant rapture with which they licked their decaying lips became a kind of ripple in the air, flowing over the three in hostile waves.

"Great Janos!" Rinda cried. "If the rain puts out our torches, the ghouls will eat us for sure!"

"Do not cast away hope, girl child!" said Guin, still fighting without sign of fatigue. Realizing that slashing at the fiends was a waste of time, he had changed his tactics, skewering them with the point of his broadsword and flinging them as far away as he could. "Fight, and hope! Are you not of the holy royal family of Parros?"

"Guin! My hand is nearly numb. I cannot hold on much longer." Rinda's voice was thick with despair. She was clutching on to Guin's neck with all the strength she had left, but the weight of the torch in her other hand was too much; she felt as if she must drop it at any moment. Just then, Remus screamed. He had been helping Guin, bravely driving back the creatures with the burning stick, when some torso, already cut to ribbons, came flying in from above and swept his torch away.

Fat drops of rain were hitting their faces now, and the ghouls pressed in even harder, ecstatic in the worsening weather. A violent wind blew through Rinda's hair, and Guin had to stop swinging his sword and draw back to protect his sputtering torch.

"Doal's arse!" he roared. "I know I've made it through worse than this—I'm sure of it—"

"Guin! Look!" Rinda shouted. The strange ring of fear in her voice was so strong that, for a second, Guin forgot the danger they were in and turned to follow Rinda's pointing torch with his eyes. He gave a low growl of unpleasant surprise at what he saw.

It was hard to believe. There from amidst the jagged trees came a full company of riders—their armor, cloaks, and helms so black that it seemed they had been formed out of the darkness itself. Even their horses wore black barding, with blinders on their eyes to keep them from startling. Hitting the horses' necks with short leather whips to urge them forward, the riders steadily advanced in three ordered columns.

"A search party from the keep!" cried Rinda. "Oh, Janos! We are finished!"

"No, wait," Guin muttered. The two eyes of his leopard head shone bright with a wild hope. "Just the opposite. This may be our only chance for survival—look, I think the riders and the ghouls have noticed each other!"

The horses reared and shied, refusing to go any further. None of the well-trained riders were thrown, but not a few gave shouts of fear and disgust when they saw the ghouls shuffling toward them. The fiends, rent, crushed, and cut into ribbons, squirmed like giant maggots from some pit of hell—their broken bodies growing ever more thirsty for living, unspoiled flesh.

"Look! The ghouls have found themselves a bigger meal than us," Guin growled, his shoulders heaving with every breath.

"What were those riders thinking, on a night like this with a storm coming in?" asked Rinda. "They bear the crest of Stafolos Keep on their arms; you'd think they would be more wary of the Marches."

"They've strayed too far, searching for their comrades who never came home," said Guin. "If they were so unlucky as to have lost their way in the Roodwood when night fell, then the pixies' trickery could have kept them going around in circles. But see there, they each have torches fixed to their saddles. These riders know what it means to wander in the Marches at night."

"Guin, look!" shouted Remus, clutching on to the leopard warrior's arm.

The clearing, once eerily silent, was now filled with horrified screams and the brutal sounds of battle. The riders of Gohra were accustomed to defending their land from the horrors of the Marches, and they had come prepared to face ghouls; but there were too many, for they had divided and multiplied like some fiend of Nospherus with each cut of Guin's blade. The result was catastrophic for the riders, who were still in close formation without enough room to properly swing their swords when the horde of flesh-craving ghouls flew into their midst.

Darting past the blades to land on the riders' breastplates, the ghouls crawled relentlessly upward, questing for unprotected flesh. The riders fell from their horses, screaming and clawing at the decaying flesh of their assailants, but the ghouls fastened themselves like leeches to the bare skin of the riders' faces, suffocating their prey until the riders' strength gave way and the monsters could feast undisturbed on the warm flesh.

Rinda gasped in horror and hid her face behind Guin's shoulder. Several ghouls had grasped and sucked at the flesh of the screaming and struggling men until their faces caved in; then, lusting for more, they disappeared into their victims' armor. Some riders jumped off their horses in a desperate attempt to save their fallen brothers in arms, but before they had gone more than a few paces they were already fighting to save their own lives.

"Guin—we have to save them!" Remus, the boy, had refused to cover his eyes like his sister Rinda, but now he was fighting back nausea as he stood trembling at Guin's side.

"Foolish boy child," replied Guin. "Are they not the enemy come to capture you? It's our luck that the ghouls are so taken with them. Indeed, we should be trying to escape now—though I wouldn't give us very good odds of living to see the morning if we ran into the depths of the forest now. If only the riders can hold out until the first rays of—"

Suddenly Guin interrupted himself with a howl so loud that Remus jumped back and screamed, and even Rinda shook.

"Guin?"

"I am a fool!"

"Guin! What is it? Guin?"

The warrior turned his leopard head skyward and cursed loudly. "How could I have forgotten about the corpse-eaters' cursed nature—the very thing that created our peril in the first place! They eat the flesh of beasts and men, then take the bodies for their own. Once they possess the bodies of the new riders as well, and remember us, we are lost!"

"Guin—!"

"I cannot possibly stand against so many until the morning. Arrgh! Jarn and his wisdom!" shouted Guin, thrusting both of his powerful arms into the air in a gesture that seemed both prayer and curse. But he did not stand there long—suddenly, the leopard warrior was a blur of movement.

"Guin! Guin, what are you doing?" Rinda yelped in fear.

Guin shouted over his shoulder, "Children! Give me your torches!"

"What are you doing? You'll start a brush fire! We'll all burn!"

"Better than having the living blood sucked out of us by those ghouls!" the leopard-man exclaimed, ignoring Rinda's warning and thrusting the torch he had snatched from her hand into the underbrush. "Now burn! Migel, god of fire, Dagon, god of wind, lend me your strength! Now burn, cursed forest, burn!"

The lush leaves and branches resisted Guin's blazing assault for a while, but before long there was a faint crackling sound, followed by the orange glow of flames quickly spreading through the undergrowth.

A wave of panic rippled through the dark forest. Small birds that had been asleep in the tree branches burst forth from their roosts and grass snakes hissed as they slithered frantically away from the blaze. Panic spread among both the Gohran riders and their ghoulish foes.

Soon the fire lit a wide area, bringing false day to the clearing. In a few short moments, the rule of the night was turned
on its head, and the horrible flesh-eating demons quaked and
hurried to escape, leaving their still-living prey on the ground.
The flames leapt higher and brighter still, scorching the sky,
sending the ghouls dancing in circles in a mad flight for safety.

"Guin! The heat!"

"There's no way out! It's spreading too quickly!"

The twins of Parros yelled over the crackling of the flames.
Guin stood unmoving as some great statue, his hand at his
waist, his entire body bathed in the light of the brush fire. His
cloak flowed out behind him, blown by the hot wind that rolled
out from the flames. Standing there, a giant, surrounded by
the whirling ghouls and the riders that had been transformed
into living torches by the forest blaze, Guin was like a half-beast
god, filled with a life force that shone clear and iron strong.
Rinda's voice caught in her mouth and she swallowed hard.

Surrounded by fire, the ghouls scattered and shriveled,
screaming horrible things that were not words. Like the riders,
they milled about helplessly, animated torches that did not
burn out but instead shrank and melted away like ice thrown
into a fire. Their screams of pain and curses drowned out even
the crackling of the flames and the howling of the wind, and

Rinda and Remus couldn't but join them in screaming as the wildfire blew through their hair and singed their skin.

Then, Guin moved.

Where only a moment before he had stood like a carven monument to some deity, the leopard-headed warrior now leapt into action, scooping up one of the twins of Parros in each of his powerful arms.

"Come, children!" he howled, running back up the path in the direction from which they had come, evading the fire he had created.

The fire had become a conflagration, burning into the heavens and overwhelming night with a fierce red mimicry of day. Guin wove between and pushed aside the other fleeing denizens of the wood, running tirelessly until he found what he had been searching for: the Roodspring!

"This blaze should keep the nixies from any mischief," the leopard-man growled as he plunged into the pool, not pausing to give the twins a chance to protest from their awkward position clutched beneath his arms. He kept going until even their heads were entirely underwater.

Tongues of flame sputtered and crackled at the edge of the spring, almost as though the fire were enraged at the narrow escape of its intended prey. The Roodwood had lain silent for thousands of years, nurturing dark life in its hollows—but it was

silent no longer as the fire invaded the wood, raging as if cov-
etous of the forest's heart itself.

"—Children?"

Guin's feline head, soaked and dripping, was the first to
emerge from the water. "Children, do you still live?"

Two small heads, water pouring from platinum blond hair,
emerged on either side of the giant leopard face. Rinda spit out
a mouthful of water, her teeth chattering as she replied. "We've
certainly been better, but yes, we're alive."

Guin looked around them. It was a wasteland. The
destruction wrought by the fire and the signs of battle stretched
around them on all sides.

The trees stood blackened and charred and the underbrush
had been reduced to little more than ash. The burned swath was
unbelievably wide, giving a clear view across the countless
stooped skeletons of half-burned trunks.

Seeing no immediate sign of danger, Guin strode from the
spring and then violently shook himself, spraying water all
around him just like some great cat might after a swim.

After shaking his head to cast off the last few drops of water,
Guin stretched out his hands to pull the twins up from the
spring. Brother and sister clutched onto his arms as he lifted
them out of the water, thoroughly soaked and bedraggled, teeth

chattering with cold. Though they could barely stand, the children's first act was to look at each other and hug.

Beyond the blackened husks of trees, they could faintly see the phantasmal bluish outline of a range of mountains. Over them—there!—came the first glint of brilliant sunlight. Dawn had come at last, and a welcome sight it was. And if perhaps it did not shine as brightly as it is said to have in the days of old, to the twins its blessed rays seemed to be full of an enchanting warmth.

"We...we made it! We're alive!" whispered Rinda, still hugging her brother tight, her voice half disbelief, half pure joy. "The air is so sweet! And what a bright morning!"

"The storm saved us—and twice at that," said Guin. "The wind spread the fire that rescued us from the flesh-eaters of the forest, and the rain put out that fire at just the right moment—or the spring water would have boiled, and we would have burned along with the ghouls and riders. It was a good bit of luck; we can't count on being so fortunate in the future."

"I wonder if anyone at Stafolos Keep saw the fire?"

"I don't think they could have missed it, a blaze that big. And besides, they lost at least two squads of riders to it," said Guin. "They will wait for the last patches of fire to burn out before sending a search party—by which time we should be long gone. But before that, you children need to dry off those clothes." Guin wrung out his cloak as he talked, dripping water onto the ashy lip of the spring. "And we need to eat. Else we'll not have the strength to evade any kind of search, head start or no. Thankfully, the largest oven in the Marches has just finished roasting a grand feast for us."

"My!" Rinda stared indignantly at Guin for saying such a thing—but when she saw the leopard-headed warrior standing there, looking more than ever like the half-beast god Cirenos, his outlandish features golden yellow in the morning sun, she swallowed her objections, and joined him in looking through the ashes and tree husks for small beasts that might have been caught in the night's blaze. After they saw Guin pick up his first catch and thrust it into his maw, savory-looking juices dripping from the meat, the twins lost any inhibitions they might have had and began searching and eating in earnest.

"So, what do we do now?" asked Rinda, licking her fingers with satisfaction after they had filled their stomachs, empty since yesterday, and shaken off the cold of the water.

"A good question," replied Guin, shaking his head. "I must go in search of myself, that much is clear. I need to know who I am, why I wear this mask, and whatever this 'Aurra' is."

"And us…?"

Rinda and Remus looked at each other. But before they could say anything else, the leopard-headed warrior's rueful laughter cut them off.

"Regardless of what we want to do, the order of the day is survival. I can hear a few dozen pairs of hoofbeats coming this way—a welcome party from the keep. It would seem that our time for deliberations is limited indeed."

Chapter Two

THE KEEP ON THE MARCHES

I

Above their heads, the soft blue canopy of the sky arched in every direction.

Beneath their feet, the burnt remains of the undergrowth smoldered, still warm in places from the blaze that had only burned itself out in the early morning. The morning air of the Marches tickled and filled their nostrils with the harsh smell of the woods, made fresh and pungent by the night's purifying fire and rain.

The twins, silently holding each other's hands, could tell at a glance that the thirty or so mounted warriors were Gohran. Everything they wore—their helms, armor, cloaks—was black. Even the barding on their horses was a dull black that matched the ash beneath their hooves and the skeletal husks of the trees through which they weaved their approach. The black helms were turned toward the twins, and the leading knights bore crossbows ready to send lethal shots of lead with

deadly accuracy right at the children's throats. Hiding or fleeing were no longer options, so the twins simply stood there,
saying nothing, captured.

Their distress at being discovered, however, was nothing
compared to the bewilderment of the knights at seeing the
twins and their strange companion standing there. Remus and
Rinda were like two pearls, wood spirits, with eyes the color of
the sky at dusk after the last rays of the setting sun have faded,
and platinum blond hair that shone all the more now that it
had dried from the dousing it received during the dreadful
events of the night before. Next to them, the warrior Guin
looked like a great half-beast god with his arms crossed over his
powerful chest. Had he been one of the hideous primitives of
Nospherus he would not have stood out any more. Looking at
him, even the twins, who had grown quite close to the leopard-
man after the night's adventure, and were even starting to feel a
strange kind of sympathy for him, couldn't help but think that
this great, fantastic creature was the product of some demon's
imagination.

In the morning light, he had all the presence of a king.
Gone was the dried blood and spring-muck that had covered
his battle-scarred skin when the twins first found him; and the
armor, leggings, gauntlets, broadsword, and cloak he had
picked up from the fallen soldiers from the keep gave him the

air of an ancient soldier of legend—much more than he had the
day before, when he lay by the forest pool like a piece of human
driftwood, clothed only in a crude loincloth. Rather than
obscuring his form, the armor accentuated his rippling muscles, perfectly complementing a body that seemed nonetheless
agile for all its massiveness. The tawny features of his leopard
head stood out like a golden sun against the blackness of the ash
that lay in lumps and piles around them, and his eyes shone
with the ferocity of a beast.

The knights crossed through the remains of fallen trees,
stopping in formation to cut off the path on which the three
companions were walking. All the while they stared in bewildered fascination at the bizarre sight before them. Still, the
well-trained Gohran soldiers were renowned for their
strength—one of their knights was worth a hundred ordinary
men in battle—and they had seen many strange things during
their patrols of the Marches; and so, uneasy though they were,
they kept a firm grip on their reins, their crossbows trained on
their mark. Thirty strong and confident in their strength, they
prepared for battle, but made no move to attack, awaiting the
commands of their captain, who rode in front with the long
black plume of his rank flowing from atop his helm.

The captain seemed the most intrigued of them all, and he
stared at the three for a long while before shrugging as though

shedding off a dream. Finally, he opened his mouth to speak.

"Well, well! This is a surprise. I left the keep as the sun rose this morning with orders to find the cause of the great fire in the forest and the whereabouts of our two missing squads...and to find and capture the young prince and princess of Parros, who were doubtless responsible for much of these strange events. While the cause of the fire has evaded us, we did find the bones and burnt corpses of our comrades toward the heart of the wood, and now, the Pearls of Parros. But this..." He paused, his eyes widening ever so slightly as he looked at Guin. "Never did I expect to find here, in the ruins of the Roodwood, a monster spawned from Cirenos himself. What—what the hell *is* that?"

The captain raised his ornately decorated whip and pointed at Guin, making a strange gesture—a Gohran charm for warding off demons.

Guin glared at the knights, his eyes flaring a fierce yellow. "Children," he said in a deep gravelly growl, indistinguishable from an animal's snarl to the unaccustomed ears of the Gohran men. "They have come for their friends as we knew they would. When I count to three, leap to the side. Speed is your only ally against those crossbows. I'll take the captain for my shield."

"Guin—no! Stop!" Rinda cried out, holding back Guin's arm with both hands. "There are thirty crossbows aimed at us, ready to fire at any moment! We can't fight against this many!"

"Did that beast say something?" asked the captain, his thickly accented voice filled with suspicion.

Before Guin could act, Rinda shot a glance at her twin brother, then stepped boldly forward. "Dogs of Gohra! The twins of Parros neither run nor hide. Take your pearls back to your lord at Stafolos and boast of your victory! But this man here—this warrior is merely a passer-by. He had no part in this. I ask you to take us two and us alone!"

The captain slapped his saddle and raised his faceplate to stare at her with narrowed eyes. Although Rinda was tall for her age, from atop a horse she looked quite small and insignificant; yet, her slender body was filled with bitter pride—a fierce, powerful pride that only one of high noble birth could hope to muster. So forceful was her manner that perhaps the captain actually gave her words some consideration. But then he slapped the knob of his saddle once more and with a dark, crafty smile on his lips, turned his gaze back to Guin.

"We Mongauli have lain waste to your land, young princess of Parros." His eyes narrowed further still, his voice dropping lower in a harsh provincial drawl. "I have captured you, and the Crown Prince, and for that I shall surely receive the Black Lion. But should I bring back this man—no, this *beast*—my lord will be all the more pleased. Surprising that I've not once heard even a rumor of a warrior like him—just look at those muscles! That horrendous face! If he's half as strong as he looks, he'll be a pretty prize, and if he turns out to be some trick of the demon Doal, then my lord will know best how to dispose of him. What interests me most, however, is the garb of the Stafolos Keep patrol he wears, and how he got it... Hear me now! It is my duty to bring the three of you back to Stafolos Keep, unharmed. Throw down your swords and ride on our horses, or be tied to the saddle and dragged along behind—the choice is yours."

"You would tie the twins of Parros behind your horses like the lowest of slaves?" shouted Rinda in sudden fury. Remus nervously laid his hand on her arm, but just then, the leopard-man Guin stepped forward, placing his hands on the twins' shoulders.

"Very well." Guin spoke slowly, carefully pronouncing each word so that the knights would understand him. "We will throw down our swords. We will go to your keep. Only, give these children the respect that is due to them." Then, with a strangely noble manner, Guin removed the sword from his belt, scabbard and all, and threw it down into the ashes.

At a sharp order from the captain, several of the knights dismounted and approached the three. All of them were noticeably nervous, and not a few had their fingers crossed in a

Gohran charm for warding off evil. As quickly as they could, they snatched the weapons off the ground, then made their captives mount, tying firm leather bands to their wrists which they then fixed to the saddles. Rinda and Remus rode one horse together; Guin was placed on a horse of his own. Two powerfully built warriors rode close on either side of Guin's horse, the three steeds bound together by a sturdy leather cord wound through their saddles.

"Guin." The soldiers had finished securing their prisoners, and had turned the horses around to begin the journey out of the ash back toward the keep. Separated though they were, the twins were still close enough to Guin for Rinda to hiss to him in a loud whisper: "You wouldn't be in this fix at all if it wasn't for us. I—we owe you an apology."

"No apologies." Guin's stoic voice matched the fixed features of the leopard mask. "It doesn't matter. It was I who killed their brethren. I am their enemy, whether I am with you or not. More importantly—" he shot a glance at the two warriors riding silently on both sides of him, "I want you to teach me something. I might have known, once, but all my knowledge has left me. What is this Gohra? What kind of land is it? Where does it lie, is it big, is it vulnerable? Why did their land attack and conquer yours?"

"Gohra is a formidable realm that rules the eastern half of

the great and civilized Middle Country," Rinda replied in a low voice. "On the Marches where it was, Gohra used to have to painstakingly carve every new bit of land out of the wilderness. And as the only one of the Three Kingdoms to border on the Marches, it endured the constant assaults of fiends and barbarians from the outer lands, and its armies became famous for their strength and boldness. Gohra is actually more an alliance than a kingdom. It's made up of three archduchies—the Archduke Olu Ghan's realm, Yulania; the Archduke Tario's realm, Kumn; and the Archduke Vlad's domain, Mongaul, where we are now. They always used to bicker and fight among themselves; but of late they have arranged a truce of sorts to run their kingdom as a whole, knowing that, if they did not, they would all lose. They even have a common ruler, Emperor Sohl. He's the last remaining descendant of an old Gohran royal bloodline or some such; but even a child of three knows he's just a figurehead puppet that jumps when the archdukes so much as lift their fingers. Parros was a peaceful land, the richest and most beautiful realm in the Middle Country, wealthy from trade, with a long civilized history and a glorious culture second to none—the pearl of the Middle Country, the flower of the Middle Country... It was one of the Three Kingdoms, along with the new, rough lands of Gohra, and the mysterious Cheironia to the north. The roads of Parros connected every city—they even civilized part of the Marches—and in the height of the Third Dynasty, workers from Parros built the Henna Highroad to protect travelers..."

Remus pitched in halfway through Rinda's history lesson. "Gohra stopped opening new land in the Marches a long time ago and started to plan their invasion of the richer lands of the Middle Country. Minister Lunan told us that the three archdukes argued about this for a long time, but in the end it was Vlad of Mongaul that gathered his troops and marched on Parros. All the Mongauli soldiers were hardened veterans, straight from the Marches patrol. Against them, Parros..."

Rinda interrupted, her voice quavering. "We were so used to peace, we never saw the attack coming! The Mongauli forces took down one fort after another along the Parros highroads, but their main host was sent up around the Parros-Cheironia border to attack our capital city from behind, killing the royal family as they lay in their beds..."

"Except for us two...right, Rinda?"

"Except for us. I still don't understand it. Cheironia and Parros were always friends. We signed treaties, and peace between our two countries prevailed for centuries. That's why Parros's northern border was so poorly defended. No matter how skilled in strategy the Mongauli archduke is, it's unthinkable that he could have attacked us from the north without

Cheironia's cooperation, or at least some sort of tacit agreement. There's no other way! The Emperor of Cheironia sold his soul to those Mongauli devils."

"And so the city fell." Guin looked at them curiously. "But then how did you two come to be here, in the Marches?"

Remus made to answer but his sister cut him off with a "Shh!" Then with an odd expression on her face she looked at the black knights riding in tight formation around them and barely more than mumbled, "Stranger things have happened to the royal blood of Parros."

As they talked, the riding party had left the Roodwood. Now they came to a place where the tree branches opened and Stafolos Keep was revealed above them.

They were in the midst of a deep sea of trees, with only an occasional island of meadow or hillock. The rushing sound of a river had been growing louder as they made their way slowly upward, and now they could see it snaking away behind the rise where the keep sat. Beyond the forest, mountains rose in the distance, a black range of peaks under the hazy indigo sky forming a line of dim, sinister shapes on the horizon.

They were in the highlands of the Marches now, with a good view of the surrounding land. Beyond the river there was no more forest or undergrowth, just endless rocky plains— wildlands where the barbarous tribes of the Sem made their homes. It was true that the forest hid many dangers, but in the wildlands danger was everywhere, and there was no place to hide.

Rinda shivered slightly atop her horse, remembering stories she had heard during more peaceful times in the Crystal Palace of Parros—stories of the fearful wildland tribes. But to escape this place, they would have to cross the great black waters of the Kes River, and enter that rocky, barren wilderness. If she had to choose, she would take even the Roodwood and the cruel Gohrans over the Kes and the Nospherus wildlands. Rinda sighed. Places where one could live in peace were so few these days. She made a quick sign to ward off evil, and looked up at the towering structure above her.

It was a massive fortress of hewn stone—a true Marches stronghold. Cut into the grey blocks that formed the outer wall were innumerable crossbow slits, like eyes ever watchful for wildling raids. Several towers rose inside the walls, creating a complex but beautiful symmetry. Two flags flew from each: the Black Lion of Gohra and the flag of the Mongauli archduke.

The keep stood at the end of a long, winding road that rose slowly out of the dark forest. The hillside had been cleared behind the keep so that watchers on the walls could see all the way down to the bottom of the valley where the swift waters of the Kes flowed. Towering over the forest trees, with the deepening purple of the mountain range in the distance, the keep seemed infused with a kind of Marches gloom, wrapped in an enduring silent chill.

As they drew nearer to the keep and the gates loomed ever higher, a dread quiet fell over the black knights and their prisoners. Barely daring to breathe, they guided their horses onward in a slow and silent walk. A black snake cut across the rocky path ahead of them; a strange black bird flew up from the forest with a cry that sounded unsettlingly like a human scream...but no one seemed to notice. A short way up ahead the stone walls of the keep towered—the end of the road, and the end of the twins' hope for escape.

"Hail, gatekeeper! Open the gates!" the captain's voice echoed in the silence below the walls.

A watcher peered from one of the embrasures; then, with a great grinding noise, the tall gate slowly began to open. The black horses and their knights were just passing through the archway when—

"No! I will not pass through this gate!" Rinda's cry rang out loud and harsh.

Startled, Remus grabbed her shoulder from behind to quiet her, but she shook him off. Her deep, violet eyes, wide with fear, were fixed on the towering fortress above them.

"Silence! What's the meaning of this?" the captain barked,

guiding his horse back down the line at a fast trot. Rinda was shaking her head, still staring at the keep.

"A plague rides on the air here. The smell of rot! This is Doal's realm. Can't you feel it? The keep is doomed, don't you see? No, I will not pass through this gate. There is a disease in there I will not touch."

A shiver ran visibly through the soldiers. There was fear in the superstitious hearts of the Marches patrol. They remembered the recent demise of their fellows and the terrible fire in the Roodwood, and even the boldest among them felt that the leopard-headed creature they had found was no good omen. They knew that the royal family of Parros was first among the priests of Janos, that their bloodline had given rise to some of the greatest prophets and holy men in history. And they knew that it had been their brothers who had put the royal family to the blade.

Now a whisper rose up among the men as they paused between the large outer wall gate and the entrance to the inner keep. "'Tis the curse of the royal house!" A few of the soldiers made the sign of Janos over their breastplates.

"Ehyah! What's this talk?" the captain spat and rode forward along the line again, whipping the rump of each horse he passed by with his lash. "Keep moving! Is this not the same Stafolos Keep we left at daybreak this morning? We may be near the perils of the Marches out here, but inside is Mongauli territory and safety! Nothing fiendish can pass through these walls! If anything unpleasant happens, it will be because we tarried in delivering these cursed twins of Parros. Now, ride! Our lord is waiting."

The knights exchanged glances, then slowly urged their horses forward.

Guin looked at his small companion with some curiosity, but Rinda had fallen into a determined silence. She clutched Remus's hand, and burying her chin in the leather collar of her jerkin, she rode silently forward among the dark knights. Only, her alert eyes looked out from behind the silver hair half-covering her face, and it seemed they shone with a strange violet light. But soon they too were hidden as her dark eyelashes lowered.

Thus the company entered Stafolos Keep.

—— 2 ——

"Rinda?" Remus whispered, looking fearfully at their surroundings. "Will they kill us?"

"How would *I* know?" Rinda snapped. Then, regretting her temper, she added, "But even if they are to kill us, they will first send us to the Mongauli capital, where we'll be tried by the Archduke himself, I should imagine. Have courage, Remus, and don't slouch so. We are the last of the Parros royal family; we will at least act the part."

The vaulted ceiling high above them was made of the same cold ocher-yellow stone as the walls. Small windows were set so high in the walls that even in mid-day the interior of the keep was enveloped in gloom—a thin darkness that seemed cold against their skin.

"I smell mold." Rinda screwed up her face as she walked. They had dismounted and the knights were now bringing them down a long hallway; one pushed her ahead. "Mold and bewitchment. I would rather die than live in a Marches castle."

Nearby, Guin gave a low growl in agreement.

"We didn't join no Marches patrol on account of wanting to be here either, lass," grunted the black-garbed soldier closest to Rinda. "'Tis a three-year trial, and I tell ye: it be enough to scare even the boldest Mongauli youth to the very core—not that most would admit it. Aye, they say a Mongauli goes to the Marches a child, and comes back a man—but there's more than one keep in the Marches. A lad with coin in his sleeves might buy a fine post at Talpho Keep, only a day's ride from the city streets of Torus, or somewhere along the Henna Highroad—Fort Eiem, maybe—and spend his days checking merchant loads and lining his pockets with bribes. Unlucky bastards like me get sent out here to Stafolos or to Alvon where you can't so much as get out of bed without stepping on a faerie, and those blasted Sem can stroll up and attack us whenever the mood strikes 'em."

"Give your tongue such freedoms and you're likely to lose it!" The captain appeared suddenly by their side and gave the soldier a loud crack on the shoulder with his lash. The man winced and fell silent, concentrating on matching his steps to those of the man beside him as they continued along the stone corridor.

The corridor was long, so long that Rinda thought it would

never end; and it was dark, and chilly, and the sounds of their footsteps and voices echoed ghoulishly. Set in the walls on either side of the hallway were carved forms of gods, their bodies and faces worn so smooth that it seemed they had been there since before time began. Perhaps there were hidden doors in the faceless black stretches of wall between the statues.

Spending a night in this horrid place is going to be as bad as sleeping hidden in the vasya thickets back in the Roodwood, thought Rinda, hugging herself tight with her arms to stop the shivers running through her body.

They turned a corner, went up a stone stairway, and then turned again. It was so silent that Rinda thought the keep deserted—until they turned yet another corner and the hallway suddenly opened up into a large hall, split at regular intervals by many stone columns. There they saw many men and women, servants perhaps, moving about hastily.

The company walked through the midst of the hall, heading toward a dais in a large alcove that was cut into the far wall. Thin pillars stood in a line between this alcove and the main hall, and visible inside were a large table and several chairs. The chairs were not placed across from each other in such a way that they might encourage friends to sit and converse, but rather were set with their backs to the wall, the table between them and the chamber, likening the table to a judges' bench, and the hall

a courtroom. Atop the table were a wine jug, a stone goblet, and a plate, all made of stone. In fact, the table and the chairs, too, were made of stone with thick furs atop the seats for comfort. Sunk deep into the fur of the central chair sat a large man.

"Reporting, your Excellency." The captain stopped the company before the dais and took off his plumed helm, holding it to the left side of his chest. "I bring three captives, taken from the ashes of the Roodwood."

"Those children, they are the twins of Parros, yes," replied the seated man in a slow, measured voice. "But what, captain, is the strange one beside them?"

As she listened to the captain, still standing with his helm to his chest, relate the events leading to the discovery of Guin and the twins, Rinda's attention focused on the man he was addressing.

He sat in the largest of the chairs in the long line behind the table—almost a throne, so big it was. The chairs to either side were in pairs, each successive pair with shorter backs than the previous pair. It seemed that they were there for the keep-lord's family, or trusted retainers, perhaps, to sit for formal audiences; but at present all were empty, save for the skins that hung on each, waiting expectantly for their occupants' return.

Watching him as he sat with his elbows resting on the stone table, with the chairs as his only companions, Rinda could tell that the man on the dais was quite tall. But it was quite impossible to say how old he was or even what his face looked like because he, too, wore black armor, black boots, black gloves, a long black cape, and a great black helm. Only the silver crest adorning his breastplate set him apart from the soldiers that had captured them.

More startling still was that, while the soldiers' mouths and chins were visible below their faceplates, the man in the chair wore under his helmet another mask made of black cloth, so that not one inch of his skin touched the outside air. Rinda judged from the tone and depth of his voice that he was a man in the middle of his years, but her eyes could tell her nothing more about him.

"...and so, my lord, I have brought this creature before you for your study and disposal, as you see fit."

While Rinda had been engaged in guessing the nature of the man behind the table, the captain wrapped up his report, and bowing deeply, took a few steps backwards. The dark figure was surely the lord of this place, and now the captain appeared to be waiting for further orders, but no words were forthcoming from the keep-lord's mouth.

One of the black gloves slid across the tabletop and picked up the stone goblet. Expecting him to take off the mask, Rinda's eyes went wide; but he seemed to reconsider, and setting the goblet down again, he rapped the gloved hand against the table.

"Never have I seen such a creature! Third Captain, this leopard-man wears the armor of the Stafolos Keep patrol. Why?"

"My lord, I believe he took it from one of the men in the fifth squad."

"I see." A black-gloved hand irritably rapped the stone surface again. "Take the armor off him, and then that mask. Then we shall see if he is truly a leopard-headed god, or a fool with a leopard mask stuck on him. Rip it off, if you must."

"Yes, my lord."

Rinda panicked for a moment, fearing that Guin would forget they were totally surrounded and go wild as he had in the forest; but the leopard-man held himself back. All he did was give a low, guttural growl as the men approached him; he was quiet as they cautiously went about removing his cloak and armor.

Soon, Guin looked much as he had when the twins first met him in the Roodwood, wearing only a leather loincloth and a broad leather baldric that ran diagonally across his chest. With both hands tied behind his back, he stood proudly before the lord of Stafolos Keep.

The execution of the keep-lord's second order, however,

did not go as smoothly. Mask or not, the leopard head was so tightly fixed to his shoulders that, try as they might, the men could not pull it off. When one of the soldiers, with a look of determination in his eye, pulled out a short sword, Rinda put a fist to her mouth and screamed.

"No—hold." The keep-lord raised a hand to stop the soldier. "I have seen enough. He is a true leopard-man. Do not harm him. I will decide what to do later. I have never heard of a creature such as this that was no evil spirit, but flesh and blood... Interesting. I will examine him further, below, not here. As for these children—these are the Pearls of Parros?" The face, half-covered by the great black helm, moved slightly as his gaze turned to the twins. Rinda's body shivered slightly, and she felt Remus grip her arm to comfort her.

"I am the Count Vanon, given this keep at Stafolos by the orders of His Grace, the Archduke Vlad of Mongaul."

He had only barely finished his introduction when Rinda shouted in terror. "Vanon! *The* Black Count of Mongaul?" She began flailing against the soldiers, who roughly pushed her closer to the table.

The black-garbed man laughed. His laughter was eerie and hollow, like a wind howling in the depths of his armor. "Has the name of the Black Count of Mongaul, and word of the plague he carries, spread all the way to Parros in the Middle

Country, then?" he said slowly, and laughed again.

"Have no fear. For no other reason have I wrapped my body tight than that no air or human gaze might reach it. Even so, Archduke Vlad thought me unsuitable for his palace halls, and so he made me lord of my own keep, out here on the northern edge of the Marches. Perhaps His Grace thought I would be less lonely out here, this close to my freakish brethren across the waters of the Kes." Though she could not see through the mask, Rinda could swear she heard a cruel smile in the count's voice. "Tell me, my dear, would you like to see the face of the Black Count? It could make a good tale someday! Your leopard-man companion may be freakish to the sight, but he has more claim to the title of 'human' than I, I'm afraid. It is all I can do to keep..." The count lowered his hand, his laugh a hollow wind behind the black helm.

"Do not worry," he said after a moment. "My disease rides on the air, so I take great pains to stay covered at all times. This is how I prevent the plague from spreading to the soldiers that share my keep. And now, my twins—"

The count rose from his chair. His movements seemed terribly slow and pained, but when he stood fully, with one hand on the table for support, he was remarkably tall. "Relegated as I have been to a life of obscurity here in this keep on the Marches, I was quite surprised when I received word—

both by fire beacon and by swift horse from Talos Keep—that
the twins of Parros had fled into my domain, and that I was to
capture them at all costs. For the beacons had told of the fall of
Parros at the hand of my lord, the archduke, only four days ago!
I ask you, how could one come all the way from the crystal city
in the very middle of the Middle Country to the lands of
Stafolos Keep in a mere two days? Surely it is a feat beyond the
skill of any mortal folk—unless they wielded the ancient dark
magic, no? And still another report came along the fires: the
Crystal Palace had fallen, yet the rumored treasure of Parros
was nowhere to be found. I heard as much from my own swift
messengers as well, so I know it to be true. Consider this:
Parros is an old country, with a history several times longer
than that of Cheironia, and dozens of times that of Gohra. Let
us assume its rulers had wisdom to match their longevity. No
matter how unready they were for the onrush of the Mongauli
armies, Parros was not so weak that it would fall into rubble in
the matter of a day and a night." The count paused. "Twins of
Parros, I shall send you to the Mongauli capital of Torus as per
my orders. Yet it is my good fortune that I have captured you
alive, for now I shall have both my reward, and the secrets of
your crystal city!"

"There are no secrets in Parros!" Rinda yelled, her face
turning pale.

"I say there are."

"There are none!"

"Then how do you explain two children traveling all the way from the crystal city to the Roodwood in the span of one day? Did you fly through the air?"

"You said yourself just now that with dark magic such a feat is possible."

"Then show me your magic!"

"Never!" Rinda's features grew haughty with queenly defiance.

"You are bold, little girl," said the Black Count, with his eerie laugh. "But there is much you do not know. Things there are in this world that are hard to withstand...and there are men in this world, little girl, that will do anything to get what they want."

"Torture," Rinda scowled. She had grown calmer, or at least she was making a great effort to appear so. "Do to us what you will, then. Fire or water, it matters not. We are the last surviving members of the royal house of Parros...all the better that we perish along with the pride of Parros! I would sooner bite off my own tongue than prolong my life in shame. I will die fulfilled, knowing that the knowledge and the glory that was Parros dies with me!"

"You are a born queen, little girl," said the Black Count.

Rinda shook her long platinum blonde hair aside and
defiantly thrust out her little chin. "Until the moment I die
upon the torturer's rack I will be a princess of Parros, true
inheritor of the holy bloodline, daughter of the noble and
great Aldross the Third—Rinda Farseer. And Remus is the
Crown Prince, the last of his line, and the one true ruler of
Parros since the day a Mongauli spear took our lord father.
Look upon yourself as you stand before us and know shame!"
Rinda concluded in a harsh tone; then, turning to her flustered
brother for support, almost irritably pushed him forward.

"Th-That's right!" Remus said, managing to give his voice
some dignity. The soft curve of his faintly trembling chin made
him look much the child next to his royal sister.

The Black Count laughed. "It seems that of the two Pearls
of Parros, one comes wrapped in a softer shell! I think the
secrets of Parros might be quite easily pried from a shell as soft
as this! But, alas, perhaps my disease is to blame, for in my
years, I have become a twisted man, and it is in ripping the
gleaming prize from the unwilling grasp of the harder shell that
I find true joy. I believe I told you there are things in this
world—things that not even you can withstand. Did I not?"

The count began moving, walking stiffly as though he had
taken an injury to the knee, coming down from the stone dais
toward them. "Think of this festering body, wrapped in band-

ages—this body that disease has made little more than a living mass of rotten flesh—lying atop yours in my bed, smothering you, caressing you, my decaying lips upon your own. How would you feel if I grabbed you by the hand and pulled you close, vile ichor painting every inch of your smooth skin black?"

Rinda couldn't put her hand to her mouth quick enough to stifle a shrill scream as she stumbled backward.

"I am sure that mere fire, the glowing hot kiss of the iron, or the lash of the whip would not be enough to break a soul like yours, my little princess of the Middle Country. But can your exquisitely pure heart bear the assault of flesh that rots even as it lives, or the dripping, staining filth that suppurates from my wounds? Do you think that, bound to my bed, you could keep yourself from screaming out all of Parros's deepest secrets?"

The count slowly reached out toward Rinda, stepping closer. But even before he had started to move, Rinda recoiled in abject fear, screwing her eyes shut and covering her face with her hands.

"Stop it! Stop it! Stop!"

The count stood still for a moment, looking at Rinda's skin, now gone whiter than paper, and he laughed quietly, the evil in his voice palpable.

"Now you see that there are things in this world that even

you cannot withstand. It is not well for children to speak so boldly of things they do not comprehend. Regardless, I will soon have the secrets of Parros from your lips, willing or no. That is to say, until I learn what I want to know, I will not send word by the fires that you have been captured. I want to be and I shall be the first to hear the secrets, to know what has befallen the great city's treasure. But I have spoken too long. This disease I bear, it likes not the touch of light, sound, or air—and so I spend much of my day in a black tower built only for me. No doubt, my own men would find it disagreeable were I to loiter about the grounds. Thus it is only for a short time each day that I come down to the main keep, and today, that time is up. Third Captain?"

"Yes, my lord?"

"Lock these three up in the tower—not my tower, but the rooms in the white tower where we keep the other prisoners. Bring them food and water, and set extra guards to ensure they do not escape. I place them entirely in your hands, captain. And that leopard-man, is he not of particular interest to you, as he is to me?"

"It is as you say, my lord."

"Indeed, I have many questions for him. Who is he, from whence did he come, what lineage or magic gave him such a visage? And, do you not think, captain, that if his muscles are as mighty as they look, and if inside that fearsome head there rests the cunning intellect of the animal he so resembles, this man would be worth his weight, nay, ten times his weight in gold, here within the borders of Mongaul? You have heard of the Archduke Vlad's plans for raising interest in armed service? Tourneys—to be held several times a year, at different locations all over Mongaul, and with phenomenal rewards to those warriors who prove themselves winners. Take care not to accidentally kill, wound, or even weaken him with starvation, my good captain. A half-beast, half-man warrior—what a crowd that will draw! I have a mind to test the mettle of our captive, and soon."

The Black Count stopped, then suddenly wavered and fell, catching himself on the table. The soldiers standing in front of the table started, but not one of them moved to help him. No one wanted to come near the accursed man that was their lord. The Black Count caught his breath, then spoke, coughing.

"I return to my tower. Take these three away, and make preparations for later. I say again, do not let them escape, and do not kill them. Tonight, in the lower chamber, we shall see how this leopard-man fights. That is all."

The captain gave a quick "my lord" and put his hand to his chest in salute. As soon as he had done this, the Black Count swayed again, then collapsed into his chair. It seemed he had also triggered some sort of secret mechanism as he did this, because as soon as he sat, the wall behind him began to pivot and the floor beneath him began to rotate on a hidden axis, all slowly turning until only a bare wall remained where the count and the great stone chair had been.

It occurred to Rinda that perhaps this was another way that Vanon countered the spread of his disease—taking even his own chair with him when he went. She had also noticed that of all the henchmen and followers of the count who were in the keep, there were none who came near him; he had no personal servants. No doubt this was why Stafolos Keep felt so deserted. From fear of their lord's black plague, soldiers and servants alike kept to their own quarters when duty did not demand their presence in the keep proper.

"One more thing..."

A strangely resonant voice that seemed to come from the very floor they stood upon broke Rinda's train of thought. She whirled around, looking for the source of the voice, but she noticed that the soldiers around her didn't seem startled in the least. It was then that she noticed a covered tube, cleverly concealed between two floor tiles. A message-pipe! Certainly it was this from which the voice had come.

"The princess of Parros seems tired. Give her a room in the tower to herself."

"What?!" *You can't take me from my brother!* Rinda wanted to scream, but the message-pipe fell silent, and the soldiers began leading the three away.

"Rinda! They're going to split us apart!" shouted Remus, struggling against the rough grip of the captain. Guin stopped him with a voice like a howl.

"Be still, it's no use! Be patient. Our lives have been extended for the time being, be thankful of that, and save your strength."

"But, but we've never been separated, never since we were born!"

"Get used to it," replied Guin. They were once again pushed along the stone corridor, then up a steep stair toward the white tower. The twins trudged despondently, growing more worried with every step.

The tower, too, was made of stone, and filled with the same chilly, clinging air as the halls below. Their path took them outside briefly, then back inside the tower walls, winding up a long spiral stair so narrow they could only walk two abreast. At last they paused at a broad landing with stone doors on either side. The captain shouted out a command that the room where the boy and the leopard-man would be kept be opened.

A jailer arrived, wearing a turban, moving slowly with his back so bent that Rinda wondered if he had been somehow crippled. He opened the nearest of the stone doors. Guin hunched over and walked into the dim chamber beyond on his own, but Remus turned and reached out pleadingly for Rinda, until the guards forced him into the room and swung the heavy door shut behind him, cutting the two off from each other for the first time in their lives.

The captain gave orders for a rotating watch, and told the jailer to put Rinda in the opposite room.

"Ooh, I don't suppose that's such a good idea, no no." The jailer protested. "Why just the day before, his Excellency the count himself put a young demon in there, to wait until he had time for an execution, you see."

"What, so it's still in there?" The captain scowled, flustered. "What of the other cells?"

The jailer smiled, revealing a mouth of yellowed, dirty teeth.

"For a young lady, now, methinks the smallest chamber at the very top of the tower would be nice."

"The tower top?" The captain seemed to hesitate; then, making up his mind, he motioned for Rinda to continue climbing the stairs.

The captain's uncertainty and the jailer's cruel laugh put Rinda on edge. What could be waiting for her up there? But it wouldn't do to show weakness before these hinterland barbarians. Keeping her chin up and her eyes forward, she headed up the increasingly steep and narrow stairs before the captain had a chance to push her from behind.

The door to the small room at the top of the stairs opened with a creak, revealing only darkness beyond, and releasing a foul smell of mold. Rinda bit her lip, and stepped inside. The door slammed shut, and the sound of the key turning in the lock echoed behind her.

"Strong girl." She heard a muffled voice say from beyond the door. Rinda shut her eyes, trying to adjust them to the darkness. "But one night in there and she'll be crying and begging for the count's mercy, heh!" They laughed scornfully; Rinda thought that they must be letting themselves be overheard on purpose, to scare her. Then she heard their footsteps retreating back down the stone stairs. The girl hugged herself tightly, and slowly opened her eyes.

She drew in a sharp breath. She could feel the blood drain from her face and a shiver run up her spine. Something was squatting there in the gloom, looking up at her with serpentine eyes from an unseen face that hovered just above the floor—fierce, savage eyes, burning with a green incandescence in the darkness.

— 3 —

Remus blinked in the dim light of the chilly prison cell. The only light trickled in through a small aperture set high in the wall. As his eyes adjusted to the dark, the features of the room became apparent: various furnishings haphazardly scattered about, chairs with skins thrown over them, a water jug atop a small desk. It seemed that their captors were not out to make their stay needlessly uncomfortable.

"Guin?"

From outside, Remus could hear the heavy bar on their door being lowered, followed by footsteps receding down the stairs.

"Guin? Why did they take Rinda away from us? Is she all right, do you think?"

Guin had been taking advantage of his extraordinary height to peer out of the high window on his tiptoes, but there was nothing to see but the dusky forests of the Marches stretching in all directions, with the barren wildlands beyond, the purple mountains forming a distant backdrop. The scenery was split into two halves by the inky flow of the Kes River. It was a deso-late view that gave no comfort. The one area of the forest that seemed lighter than the surrounding woods was doubtless the area where the Roodwood had burned the night before.

"I don't know," said Guin, turning away from the window.

"But..." Remus's eyes grew more anxious, and he rubbed his hands together nervously.

"You cannot help her by worrying about it, so don't," Guin growled. "Your sister is brave. She can deal with most things."

"But that horrible Black Count—" Remus began, but sud-denly slapped his hand to his mouth.

"What is it?"

"What's that noise?"

"Just the guards walking outside."

"No, it was something else!" Remus tilted his head, listen-ing intently, then pointed at the left wall of the chamber. "It's coming from over there. Listen, there it is again!"

Guin looked, but he could neither see nor hear anything unusual in the direction Remus was pointing. He turned back toward the boy with a doubtful shrug of his shoulders. Remus, eyes wide as a torris hare's, grabbed his arm and pointed at the wall again.

"Hear that? It sounds like...something scratching at the wall!"

"Hmm..." Guin responded, now noticing the strange noise.

"What is it?"

"Torq rats, maybe."

"But..."

Guin had marked before this that, even though they were called the twin Pearls of Parros, there was a great difference between Remus and his sister. Perhaps his sister's assumption of the role of leader had dampened his spirit, made him used to following, but it seemed that the young boy was indeed a great deal more shy, delicate, and impressionable—a young bird that had yet to shed its last downy nest feathers.

Guin laughed. "There's nothing that mere rats—" but then he abruptly broke off too and looked at the wall, his eyes narrowing in suspicion.

The scratching sound, like something gnawing on the wall with sharp teeth, had stopped, and now a loud thumping sound like something hitting the wall from the other side had begun. Guin's eyes shined as he stared at the wall, and he seemed not to notice Remus's hands grabbing on to his waist.

"That is no mere torq rat." Guin growled so low Remus could barely hear him. "Not unless the giant rats of the Marches have some sort of fiendish intelligence to match their size. Torq rats might gnaw at a wall, but I've never heard of one pounding on a wall to send a message to someone on the other side."

"Guin," Remus whispered, "maybe there's someone in the next cell."

"Ah," said Guin, and there was no need for him to say more, because at that moment, a part of the wall that they had been watching gave way, and a chunk of rock popped out and fell into their cell.

Guin reached out his arm and snatched the rock out of the air before it hit the floor, lest it make a thud that would attract the guards' attention. Then, through the small, inches-wide hole from which the stone had been dislodged, they heard the sound of stifled laughter.

"Finally." The man's voice coming from the other side of the wall was young and spirited, with a little cockiness and mischievousness thrown in. "Now we've a fine window for talking."

Remus's eyes opened wide and he looked as though he was about to say something, but Guin put his hand on his shoulder and pulled him back up against the wall to the side of the opening, and waited. He would not let down his guard until he was sure this was not some trickery of the Black Count Vanon.

Hearing no response from their room, the voice on the

other side of the wall became doubtful. "Hey! Hello in there!" Whoever it was, he sounded a little impatient. "You mean to tell me there's no one there? But that doesn't make sense, does it? Just a bit ago, when I was dozing, I woke up to a great many footsteps coming up the tower, and the racket of men walking in their armor. Then *your* door opened and shut, and the lock came down with a crash—that's what really woke me up. So speak up, I know you're in there!"

Guin and Remus looked at each other. Guin remained suspicious; but nothing about the voice—although it sounded irritable and perhaps a bit arrogant—suggested that the speaker meant any harm to anyone. "Hey! Can't you hear me? Or are you scared, and not talking? Or did you just get through one of that rotting freak's special torturing sessions, and lack the strength to talk? If that's the case, then just groan for me! Or perhaps you're waiting for me to make my introductions. Fine, then, I know my manners, and it's common knowledge by now that I stood right before that creepy keep-lord in all his rotting pestilence and told him what I thought of him—losing my armor and sword and getting thrown in here as a result. My name's Istavan, Istavan of Valachia. I was a mercenary in Torus only a few days in the Mongauli army when they sent me out here to this graveyard. Listen, I don't know what matter of man you may be, but this Stafolos Keep—this is no place for the living."

"What do you mean?" Guin, forgetting himself, rejoindered. He tried to speak as clearly as he could, but when the voice on the other side of the wall spoke again it was filled with suspicion.

"Ah, there is someone there! But what a voice! Could you be one of the witless giants of Taluuan in the north? Or a Lagon barbarian, a demon of Nospherus? You speak as though your mouth was full of the raw flesh of your enemies! Well, no matter what you are, you don't want to be in here. Even if the lord of the keep wasn't a pus-filled heap of decaying flesh, I mean. I've been a mercenary since I was twelve years of age, and I've seen my share of bastions and battlefields; I've lived in places no better than a pig sty, I have. But these cold walls, they—hey, I told you who I was, now it's your turn. How did you end up getting thrown in here?"

"My name is Guin." Guin made a great effort to pronounce every word as clearly as possible. "I was taken in the Roodwood by knights from the keep, and now it seems that the Black Count would have me fight for him in the tourneys in Torus."

"It makes sense," said Istavan, his voice regaining some of its earlier friendliness. "That old pus-bag is set on making his fortune wagering on the slaves he's always collecting. You're not in such a different position from us mercenaries. You haven't, er, promised your sword to the Archduke of Mongaul, have you?"

"I have promised my sword to none but myself, as far as I know."

"That so? Then I'll let you in on a secret. Look, I'm getting out of this accursed keep soon, like tonight, and if you know what's good for you, you'll escape when I do, too. If you don't, mark my words: you'll have every accursed stone in the place coming down on your head."

"What do you mean?" Guin put his hand lightly on Remus's shoulder to calm him, motioning for him to sit against the wall beside him. Then Guin pulled up a chair next to the hole, and sat with his legs crossed.

"This keep is cursed, that's what!" the mercenary continued, rather cheerily. "I've lived off the scraps of war since I was a lad of four, and when I was twelve, I pilfered me a suit of armor and became a man, a mercenary, in my own right. That's why when I say I've got survival instincts honed to the point of supernatural clarity, you'd best believe it. They got to calling me 'the Spellsword,' you know, on account of my surviving like magic no matter what hell-spawned horror awaited in the deadliest of battlefields. That's why you'd better listen when I say there's a demon haunting this keep. Aye, the dark clouds of misfortune are sweeping in to cover these halls even as we speak.

Maybe the pestilence comes courtesy of the bandaged keep-lord, or maybe he's just a part of some larger, darker evil. Be that as it may, Guin, the place is cursed. I heard it whispered in the mercenary quarters often enough: nobody knows what's going on in that black tower. Even the count's personal guards dare not go near the place. But one thing's for certain—there is *something* going on in there, and what that something is...well, I'm in no hurry to find out!"

"There is some proof?" said Guin with great interest.

"Aye, that there is, and coming from the count's personal tower guards no less," Istavan Spellsword replied. "It happened just before I first arrived here with my squad. It seems that the three youngest of the tower guards just disappeared within the space of three weeks. All were last seen near the entrance to that black tower. Then horses went missing, then servants on duty, then even the old steward who had served Count Vanon faithfully for years, even after the count was sent out to his exile in the Marches. It was right after the steward vanished and the rumors started to fly, that the black knights began going out on secret missions, a different group each time. The knights would leave at dawn and return at dusk, with two or three other figures riding between them, covered in cloaks. Of course, as soon as the secret missions began, the strange disappearances at the keep stopped, just like that...and there wasn't a single mouth without its share of rumors as to why."

Guin said nothing.

"You know, I once heard—I believe it was a sorcerer from Torus that told me—that the only thing that eases the pain of the black plague is nothing other than the warm flesh and blood of a living human."

He paused, but still, Guin was silent.

"I may be the 'Crimson Mercenary,' Istavan Spellsword, but my supernatural sense for danger doesn't come from me sharing my soul with a demon, as some of the rumors would have it. It's just that I can see things that other people can't—or that they pretend not to see; and when the facts are spread out too thin, I can bring them together to form patterns. So how do I know the keep's not long for this world? Because the count's gone through all the sacrifices he can get from the homesteaders and hunter families living around the keep, and the last time he sent the black knights out on one of those secret missions they came back with five or six…people, if you can call them that, who weren't each of them more than three feet tall. When one happened to fall off the horse they had put him on, his gag slipped and I heard him cry out 'Alphetto! Alphetto!'"

"Alphetto?"

"The wildling god," whispered Remus. "Alphetto is the name the Sem barbarians who live in the wildlands of

Nospherus give to their god."

"By the grassy knees of the plains-god Mos!" Istavan exclaimed. "Tell me sooner if there's two of you in there!"

"Shh!" Guin clicked his tongue to silence him. "I won't go into the whys or hows, but I have been imprisoned here with a child, and another child that was with us—a girl—was taken away at the door. You may escape if you will, Istavan, but I must first save that girl."

"Guin!" Remus grabbed the leopard-man's hand. After a short while, the voice on the other side of the wall returned.

"So this girl was taken away, by herself?"

"Yes. It seems they have taken her to a room by herself."

"Then she's done for."

"Done for?" cried Remus in a panicked voice.

Suddenly, there was a sound of something like the butt of a spear being slammed into their cell door from the outside, and a guard shouted, "Quiet in there!" There was silence for a while, and then the prisoners resumed their discussion in low voices.

"Know what I think?" said Istavan, seemingly unconcerned about the guards. "They put that girl in a separate room because they're going to use her for...you know what."

"No!" said Remus, trembling. "I won't let that demon wring the blood out of my sister for one of his vile salves!"

Guin laid a comforting hand on Remus's shoulder. Istavan, on the other hand, continued talking as though he hadn't noticed or didn't care about the boy's distress.

"If that's the case, we've even less time than I thought. Aye, truth be told, I'm getting a bit nervous. You see, when I realized that it was only a matter of time before the Sem tribes came to rescue their comrades, or even take the keep in one massive bloody raid, I made a plan. I'd badmouth Count Vanon to his face, and he'd get so mad with me I'd be sent back to the capital of Torus before you could say 'Dismissed!' See, I'm no recruit. I'm just a mercenary in the Mongauli army. The only one with the authority to punish me is General Gudoh in Torus. But the problem is, I sort of overdid it…or maybe the Black Count never had a mind to follow military guidelines in the first place. In any case, instead of sending me back to Torus with the first message convoy, he pronounces me a criminal and throws me in this place. No doubt he plans to wring my blood out too and call it an execution, eh? But I'm not worried, I've been in worse before. Know ye, that Istavan Spellsword was born holding a gem in one hand. The old muse in town said that I would grow to become a great man and one day hold the reins to a kingdom in my fist, just like I did that gem. That's my destiny, see, and I believe it. Right now I might be just a mercenary with only a notch or two on my sword, but one day I'll rule this place, all of it, and no blood-sucking ghoul is going to get in my way.

"Anyway," he continued, "I'm breaking out of this place between sundown tonight and sunrise tomorrow, and you two—"

"We three have good reason not to want to die here either," said Guin, deep in thought, crouching close to the opening in the wall so his voice could be clearly heard. "Istavan, you said you've traveled around the world. In all your travels, have you ever heard of a place, or person, named 'Aurra'?"

Remus, chewing his lip nervously, looked over at Guin. It seemed as though he and his sister had been traveling with this strange man forever, as though ages had passed since he came walking out of the woods, a warrior straight out of legend, ferocious and yet at the same time strangely vulnerable, pitifully robbed of his memory, his very identity, remembering only a few words that formed vague links to his past even as they reminded him of all he had lost.

"'Aurra,' you say? I can't say I know any country or town called 'Aurra.' Sounds like a woman's name to me," the mercenary mused, happy to have this distraction from the dreariness of the cell. Suddenly, he gave a gasp and jerked away from the opening.

"By Janos' wrinkles!" he shouted, his voice suddenly high-pitched with alarm. "By Janos of the two faces! By the wisdom of the Elder and the will of the Youth! What in hell's name have I been talking to?"

Guin realized belatedly that, caught up in the conversation, he had moved to where his leopard head was visible through the opening, from which Istavan's curses now came tumbling one after the other, each more colorful and elaborate than the last.

"By the three-and-a-half curls of Jarn Fate-Weaver's tail! What manner of beast have I been talking to? The half-man god Cirenos himself, or an unborn ghoul of the Marches? Was I on the verge of clasping hands, or paws, with something more hideous than the fiends I fought on patrol? I spent time as a mercenary in the City of Cripples, Canaris, itself—but never did I see there the likes of what I see now!"

"I...I am—" began Guin, but the mercenary, changing his tone abruptly, cut him off with an urgent whisper.

"The guards, they're coming! Bringing us our evening meal, no doubt. I'll leave the question of just what you are for later if you'll be so kind as to put that stone back where it fell from. If the guards see what I'm doing, I might as well be trying to stop the mighty Kes from flowing with my two hands for all the good my escape plan's going to do me."

"Right." Guin quickly lifted the stone and set it back in

place—and just in time, because as he was moving to sit on the long bench near the wall, they heard the heavy footsteps on the tower stairs divide into two groups as they reached the landing. One paused before the chamber where the mercenary was held. Guin could hear the small window set high in their neighbor's door creak open and a rough voice shout "Dinner!" At the same time, he heard the echoing metallic noise of the bar on their own door being lifted, followed by the slow scraping sound of the door opening.

The men standing in their doorway wore the black armor of the Marches patrol, each of them holding a torch in his hands. It was then that the prisoners first realized that dusk was coming—no, it had already arrived. Their room had been dark to begin with, and now the light coming from the small high window was a dim violet. The torches cast wavering silhouettes of the soldiers and the prisoners on the stone walls of the cell, and despite the flickering torch-flames, the room was filled with the melancholy chill of the gloaming hour.

"You, come with us," snapped the captain. With his face-plate down, it was impossible to tell whether he was the same man that had captured them in the forest. "My lord wishes to test your strength and skill."

At the same time, two of the knights stepped into the room and grabbed Guin by the arms with gauntleted hands.

"Guin!" Remus cried out and started to stand, but the captain shoved him back down. Then the jailer entered the room from behind the captain and placed a plate of meat and a lump of something that looked like mashed grains on the low table, and beside it, a jug of Gohran grape wine—dinner for one.

"Only the leopard-man," said the captain, and made a motion with his hand for the captive to be taken away.

Guin, with his usual air of unconcern, allowed himself to be led out of the room. It was as if he had two faces, one of utmost calm, one of furious action; and he wore both with ease. He was like the animal whose face he wore, able to sit in silence for hours, without moving a muscle, then flying like a raging storm into battle, returning again to perfect calm when the fight was over.

Thus it was that Guin left the room with the knights in complete calm and silence. The heavy stone door closed behind them, the heavy bar dropped, and Remus was left in the cold room all alone. The knights had left one of the torches for him in a sconce on the wall, but that merely served to send creepy shadows skittering across the room, playing upon his mind until he was sure he could see demons lurking in the corners.

His friend and guardian Guin taken away, his twin sister parted from him for the first time in his life, the young crown prince of Parros rolled up into a miserable ball atop the long bench, unable to touch the food on the table in front of him. The knights that had taken Guin away had gone back down the stairs, and all was quiet, when Remus once again heard that scratching sound, then the sound of the rock being pushed carefully from the other side of the wall.

It was followed by the mercenary's voice: "Grab it from that side, will you?" Remus hurriedly reached out and grabbed onto the stone, almost falling over backwards when it slid easily out of the opening into his hand.

With the small window reopened, Remus could see by the torchlight two sparkling black eyes peering through. Then the young, rather taut face of a man came into view on the other side of the wall.

"What's wrong, kid?" whispered the mercenary, wiping the grease from his meal off his lips with the back of his hand. "They take away that leopard-man?"

"Yes," Remus answered, his voice choked with tears. "Th-The Black Count is going to make him fight, to...to test his strength and skill."

"Ahh, right." The peculiar way the mercenary spoke gave the impression of someone who feared little, and worried even less. "Well, at least it doesn't sound like they're going to kill him, eh?"

Istavan stared through the opening, checking out Remus's room by the torchlight, until he spoke wonderingly. "Hey, kid, you look miserable! Eat some of that food, I don't think our host wasted any time mixing his black plague into the gravy. If he wanted to kill us, he'd do it by sword." The mercenary grinned and pointed with his scarred finger to the plate on the table behind Remus.

"By the way you're dressed, I'd say you're no local home-steader's child. Am I right? So how did you end up hiking around with that monstrosity, and why did the black knights bother bringing you back, too, when they caught him? That crea-ture... By Doal's arse, I knew the Marches were bad, but not this bad! It's a veritable nest of fiends out here! I mean, what is he?"

"Guin's a good person," said Remus, glaring at Istavan through the peephole. The mercenary continued as though he hadn't heard the boy's protest.

"I'd eat that food if I were you. You need your strength, and if you don't want the living blood wrung out of you, you'll help me. I've pulled enough stones out of my wall here to make a way out of this cursed tower, but I've no way of getting from up here down to the Kes River without breaking my neck. Here, I want you to pass me the sheets of the bed in your room through this hole. I can't make a long enough rope to get me out of here with just the ones I've got. I mean, I could make the strips thinner, but then it wouldn't be enough to support my weight, you see?"

"The Kes River? Whatever would you do down there?" asked Remus. But he began feeding the sheets through the hole as requested.

"I haven't any plans for when I get down there, kid," said Istavan, chuckling. "All I know is that the black Kes runs right underneath these windows, and in order to get out of here, that's where I have to go. Look, you worry about eating that meat and grainball. The first thing you learn as a mercenary is that you can't do anything on an empty stomach and do it well."

Remus did as he was told, occasionally peeking into the next room to watch the "Crimson Mercenary" tearing the bed sheets into long strips with his tough fingers and teeth, then deftly winding the strips into a surprisingly sturdy-looking rope ladder. Sitting there, listening to Istavan grumble about the jailer not giving him a torch, lining up curses and spitting them out while he worked on tirelessly, it struck Remus how different his life was now, when just a few days ago he was the Crown Prince, protected and safe in the Crystal Palace. A teardrop rolled down his cheek.

The sun had sunk completely below the horizon, and the moon shone bluish-white on the treetops, and still Guin did not return. After finishing his ladder, Istavan in the other room returned to his bench and, drawing a skin over himself and saying something about conserving his strength, fell straight asleep. And where was Rinda? Outside was the Marches forest—where they had spent the last two nights—stretching black into the distance, hiding dangers and horrors unknown. Mysterious shadows flew over it.

Remus curled up on his own bench and prepared to spend a long, uneasy night alone for the first time ever in his short life. Who could have known that Jarn Fate-Weaver, with his long beard, horse's hooves, thrice-and-a-half-curled tail, and single eye that saw through to the end of time, had chosen that very moment to quietly begin turning the little wheel of his loom? For what Jarn weaves is the longest and most intricate of tapestries, and the ones who make up its pattern are always unaware that they walk on the threads of destiny.

Guin did not return; and Istavan, who had seemingly forgotten all of his plans for leaving the keep that night, was sound asleep. Black clouds, the harbingers of a great storm, wrapped around Stafolos Keep, and the dreams of the soldiers were colored with the shades of fear, as around them another night grew quietly deeper on the Marches.

— 4 —

The guards had taken Rinda from her two companions and dragged her to a small room at the top of the tower. The heavy door to her cell had swung shut with a dull thud, and she had listened to the harsh laughter of the guards receding down the stairs. After a long moment of grim despair, she had realized she was not alone.

Like the room in which her brother and the leopard-man were being held, her cell was built of solid stone; but hers lacked even a small opening to admit daylight from without, and so she could see nothing for a while until her eyes adjusted to the dark.

A moldy, disquieting smell filled the air, doing nothing to ease the young girl's already frayed nerves. To one with her gift of farseeing, the odor meant nothing less than that she was much too close to the spirit world, and that if she made one misstep in this dark place, she might cross to the other side, never to return.

Far from making any missteps, Rinda hadn't moved an inch since she was pushed into the room. She stood perfectly still with her back to the door, peering toward the middle of the room, where, from about halfway between the floor and the dimly visible outline of a tabletop, two green eyes were staring at her, shining with an unholy light.

The eyes were too big to be those of a torq rat—almost human-sized, in fact; yet they shone from a narrow space where no human could have fit. Visions flashed through the girl's mind: it was a giant man-eating centipede, or worse, one of the ghoulish Doal-spawn from their nightmare passage through the Roodwood the night before.

Rinda stood for a long time, clutching her arms to her chest, vainly trying to stop trembling. Her blue lips whispered the name of Janos, and she traced a rune in the air to ward off demons.

The standoff ended as abruptly as it had begun. Rinda had stood transfixed, staring at those eyes for what seemed like forever, until suddenly she felt that the eyes staring back were as scared—no, even more scared—of her as she was of them! She couldn't have said how she knew, but surely it was due in part to her heightened sensitivity to the spirit auras of other living things.

Rinda took a deep breath, summoned up all her courage

and stepped forward.

"Now there, don't be frightened."

Now that the silence was broken, she found it much easier to continue. "You are a prisoner here, too?"

Nothing. The eyes continued to stare at her, unmoving. She spoke a few words more, but whatever it was under the table did not seem to understand her language. And yet, just as the girl was giving up on trying to communicate and beginning to think about sitting down and getting some rest, her bright, childlike voice finally elicited a reaction. Her cellmate slowly wormed out from its hiding place and stood in front of her.

Rinda's eyes went wide as she stared at the creature before her. At first, she thought it was a child. Even standing at its full height, it only came up to her waist. Its body, however, was not that of a child, but rather had the squat torso and long arms of a monkey; indeed, it could have been a monkey, with its round face and decidedly non-human features. At the same time, there was something in those shining green eyes that suggested that this was no wild animal.

The creature's hair fell in tangled locks down its neck, and it wore a crude cloak of animal hide with a hole cut for its head. It was not all that old, that was certain. In fact, it was probably a young girl. Her skin was everywhere covered with a light coat of fur, and at her neck and wrists she wore circlets of wisteria tendrils deftly woven with pretty flowers. Somehow, the sight of the drooping petals around the little girl's neck was a great relief to Rinda.

"You were captured, too, weren't you?" the princess said. "You and me, we're the same." She pointed at her companion, then at herself. "You're one of the Sem, from across the Kes. I've heard many tales about your kind, but this is the first time I've ever met one of you in person!"

The green eyes blinked, as if the mind behind them was trying to comprehend what Rinda was saying. Then the little girl shrugged and began to chitter rapidly in a high voice.

Now it was Rinda's turn to shrug, no matter how hard she tried to make sense of the stream of chatter. It sounded like, "Suni, suni! Ssem-lacundra-leeku."

"How would a Sem who lives on the other side of the Kes become a prisoner over here?" Rinda asked, speaking as much to herself as to her companion. The only response was another round of rapid-fire chittering. Rinda considered this for a while, then decided to opt for the most basic form of communication. Pointing to herself, she said, "Rinda, Rinda."

The reply was immediate. The wildlands girl pointed at her hide-cloaked chest and spoke, a little more slowly this time.

"Suni."

Rinda pointed at herself again. "Rinda." Then she pointed

back at her companion. "Suni." This seemed to please the Sem girl.

"Suni of the Sem," said Rinda. Though they would not be able to get across much more than this by pointing, Rinda felt that they had made a great breakthrough. Seer that she was, with firsthand knowledge of the timid hearts of young and wild creatures, she sensed ever more deeply how frightened this girl Suni was. She also knew that if she made any sudden movements, or tried to touch the young Sem, the fragile understanding between them would shatter and disappear in an instant.

So when Rinda finally made up her mind to sit down on the bench, she moved excruciatingly slowly, as if she were afraid to disturb the still air itself. The wildlands girl flinched, but soon realized that Rinda meant her no harm. Still, she watched intently until Rinda was sitting. Suni remained standing, her green eyes glittering like a startled torris hare's, until she saw that Rinda was not going to move any further. Apparently satisfied, she crept to the farthest corner and sat hunched on the floor, her curious eyes still staring at Rinda all the while.

Rinda paid her little mind. The child-princess of Parros was young and bold, but also incredibly tired. She hadn't gotten a proper night's sleep during the previous night, nor during the night before it. Just when she had made up her mind to focus her thoughts on what was to come, and the welfare of her brother, the heir to the throne, she found herself feeling quite drowsy. Curling up, she soon fell into a deep sleep.

Rinda slept the sleep of a healthy, very tired girl, which is not easily disturbed by the visitations of demons or, for that matter, the rays of the morning sun. Nonetheless she woke with a start a short time later at the sound of a terrified scream followed by the din of a deadly struggle nearby. She leapt to her feet and, looking around, discovered that the girl Suni was sprawled on the floor of the chamber, fighting for her life against two giant torq rats. Doubtless the vermin had crawled from some hole in the wall in search of dinner and had chosen Suni as the main course!

The sharp fangs of the rats pierced the little girl's flesh— one on her shoulder, the other at her thigh. Torq rats are the largest of their kin, over two feet in length, and to Rinda they looked more like fierce cats than rodents. To the tiny Sem, who herself measured no more than three feet tall, they were as threatening as ferocious wild dogs were to human children. Each weighed nearly as much as she.

"Hiiih! Hiii!" Suni screamed as she desperately tried to keep the slavering fangs from her throat. "Alphetto! Hiiih!"

Rinda did not stand still for long. Frantically, she looked

about for something to use as a weapon, but finding nothing, she jumped down off the bench and with her bare hands grabbed the torq rat that was biting into Suni's shoulder. Ignoring the horrid feel of the grimy fur in her hands, she yanked as hard as she could and threw the thing against the nearest wall with all her strength. There was a wet crunching sound as the rat's head cracked against the cold stone. Its lifeless body dropped to the floor.

The other rat moved quickly, letting go of Suni and launching itself through the air at Rinda. Grabbing a nearby chair, Rinda swung it and knocked the beast out of the air. Then she gave chase, smashing at it until she felt the small animal die. A horrible shudder ran through her body.

Quickly she searched on all sides until she was certain that there were no more torq rats sneaking in. Satisfied at last, she dropped the bloodied chair on the floor and stood there, shoulders heaving. Then she noticed Suni sobbing on the floor, picked the little girl up, and hugged her to her breast.

"It's okay, now. You're okay." She patted the little girl's wild hair. She had often heard that the Sem were an unspeakably dirty and ugly folk, but Suni was neither. She smelled faintly of dried flowers and cured leather.

"Alphetto! Alphetto..." Suni sobbed. Holding on to her little companion, Rinda suddenly felt quite strong, as if she had become a great hero.

"It's all right, I took care of them." Rinda patted the Sem girl gently on the back. But then Suni suddenly brushed off her arms, fell to her knees and began kissing Rinda's booted feet. Rinda was shocked.

"Semama, rakulanee, eeni...Suni, imikul, reeku!"

"What's that Suni? I'm sorry, I don't understand."

But what Suni did next was understandable in any language. Reaching behind her neck and undoing the flowery necklace she wore, she reached up with great solemnity and set it around Rinda's neck. Then she stepped back, a worshipful look in her eyes, and placing her hand on her chest, made a respectful obeisance to her savior. The little girl's sparkling green eyes and vibrant face expressed her feelings better than any words ever could.

Rinda smiled and raised the necklace to her lips, lightly kissing it in a sign of acceptance, and she curtsied gracefully as would the queen upon greeting an honored guest. Then she waved with her hand, beckoning Suni to sit on the bench beside her.

The two girls sat side by side in the small tower room, each satisfied, feeling that they had achieved some deep level of communication. All thoughts of their predicament and their gloomy surroundings were forgotten for a while. Hand in hand, they began to talk, each more eagerly trying to understand the other's language.

Thus they sat, utterly engaged in their attempts at communication, until well past the midnight hour, when a ghastly figure soundlessly stepped into the room through a cleverly hidden secret door in the wall behind them.

The knights, garbed all in black, led Guin down the tower steps, but instead of taking him to the large audience chamber to which they had brought the three prisoners before, they pushed him further along down stairs that wound deeper and deeper into the earth below the tower. The stone steps became suddenly steeper, and water dripped from cracks in the walls, making small puddles in hollows in the rock. The staircase wound and twisted on for what seemed like forever, until it opened out into a wider corridor, dark and dank like a cellar, with columns set along the sides.

"Turn right."

The captain pointed down the right bend of the corridor with his torch. His voice sounded hollow in the chill air, and the knights walked silently, careful not to slip on the slimy floor stones, reluctant to make any noise that could be heard over the steady *drip-drip* of water falling from the ceiling. The captain's flickering torchlight shone down the corridor in front of them, startling loathsome torq rats and wandering bats and sending them skittering off to the deeper darkness where the light could not reach them.

It was clear that the knights enjoyed this journey no more than did their captive. Guin heard them whispering the name of Janos whenever a bat went flapping overhead, or cursing when one had the misfortune of running into a spider web. The captain made no effort to silence them.

Guin simply marched forward with his customary giant strides, seeming not to notice his miserable surroundings. The captive appeared more at ease than his captors.

The captain glowered at the leopard-man and made the sign of Janos as the dark corridor suddenly began to rise, returning toward the surface. They had not gone much farther, their iron boots clanging off the cold stone of the floor, when from a shadow behind one of the columns stepped a man in a long black coat, like a wandering spirit. It was with great effort that the Gohran knights swallowed their cries of fear.

"Come, this way." The Black Count Vanon spoke with a voice like a hollow grave.

He had taken off his armor and had put on in its place a large hooded cloak. Beneath it, Guin could see thin plates of iron, covering his head, face, and hands like bandages. Moving awkwardly, as if he were some kind of giant iron puppet, the count waved to the captain to follow him, keeping his distance from the knights all the same so as not to frighten them. Lurching through the gloom ahead of them, he seemed even more spectral.

"Bring the leopard-man, I have made preparations."

Following the beckoning specter, the group continued farther down the corridor. At last they entered what apparently was a large underground chamber. Aside from the familiarly styled columns supporting the roof at intervals, the room was almost entirely empty, its walls made of bare stone. The one exception was an assortment of furnishings clustered at the far end that caught the eye and sent chills down the spine of every living man in the room.

A stretching rack, a giant stone brazier, a water tank, a windlass for hanging people upside-down, a whipping post, an iron maiden, and countless other torture devices stood there like some sort of horrid display—trophies of pain. Three slaves stood shackled before them, awaiting orders with expressions that showed no emotion or hope.

The Black Count, without so much as glancing at the horrid collection, walked past with the knights following after him. Guin strode by the devices of torture, seeming unconcerned, pretending to ignore the cloying stench of blood that filled his nostrils. Deep down inside, he was quite happy that he was not to experience the many cruel features of the count's playthings, at least not today.

It seemed his current destination lay elsewhere. The group followed the Black Count to the far wall, where he stopped before the rock face, laid his hand upon a certain stone, and pushed. The wall split into two halves, creating a short passageway that opened into a large, featureless room beyond.

This new room had neither rack nor executioner's stand, but what it contained seemed somehow more horrible than either of those things. An animal whine rose from its sole occupant, a creature which stood caged behind iron bars toward the back of the room, its eyes blazing.

"One of the giant simians of Gabul—a grey ape!" said the captain in a voice barely above a whisper, quickly glancing to either side and making the sign of Janos across his breast.

If Guin had not been robbed of his memory, if he knew just how deadly were the grey apes of Gabul, he would not have had to look upon the fangs thrusting from its maw, the knotted muscles of its two powerful arms that could rend a man limb from limb with ease, or the small eyes that burned as though all the demons of hell made their nests within its head, to see that he was doomed. Like all the creations of Doal, the grey ape was a man-eater, with a terrible fondness for playing with its food before ripping and tearing the life from its hapless prey.

But Guin had the benefit of ignorance. All he saw there was a giant, violent beast—a formidable opponent, surely, but a dirty, lowly creature, too. And even if the sight of the creature had terrified him, the leopard mask remained stoic, hiding his reaction from his captors. Some of the knights made the sign of Janos, but others, seeing Guin standing unaffected by the sight before him, felt the stirrings of awe, and not a little distaste at their comrades' evident cowardice. A knight spat on the stone floor.

As for the Black Count, he seemed rather pleased with his captive's reaction to the foul beast.

"Into the hall, prisoner." The count pointed down the stairs that led to the broad stone floor before the ape's cage.

Guin slowly looked to both sides, as though contemplating whether his chances were better going along with the count's fiendish plans, or simply flying into a rage then and there against the twenty or so knights. The count stepped back, startled, and the knights turned, threatening Guin with the sharp points of their spears. Guin hunched his powerful shoulders and, avoiding the spears, resumed walking down the stairs.

Seeing the warrior's acquiescence, the count pushed a spot on the wall again, and the stairs behind them rose up to form a wall, effectively preventing anyone from exiting the chamber. The count pressed another hidden panel, and a small wall rose from the floor between where he stood and the main chamber, creating a sort of gallery as in a coliseum.

"Prisoner. I am going to open the ape's cage in a few moments," Vanon announced in a deep voice, taking an hour-glass from the folds of his robe and placing it atop the partition wall. "Survive three turns of the glass with your bare hands, and I will throw you a short sword. Survive two more turns, and a broadsword will be yours. The better a warrior you prove to be, the better your chances of survival, for I am a fair lord, and I value a strong fighter. And know this: if you should kill the grey ape with your bare hands alone, I will give you your weight in silver as a reward. Now, show me how you do battle, leopard-man!"

The Black Count slowly pressed a final button, and with a loud creaking noise, the gate of the iron cage began to rise.

The great ape of Gabul peered about, disoriented in its newfound freedom. It howled—and then its violent, bloodshot eyes fell on the leopard-headed warrior.

Breathing heavily with anticipation, the great ape turned toward him. There was no escape. Guin would have to fight.

Chapter Three

THE DAY OF THE SEM

I

The grey ape of Gabul towered like the spawn of a nightmare. Its giant body, except for its great bald head, was covered with grimy, matted fur. Its arms hung down to the floor; its eyes glared at the leopard-man before it. Tall though he was, Guin found himself looking up at the creature, which stood a full head taller.

Guin waited with his arms relaxed, looking no more concerned than a guest at a palace tea party, calmly observing the grey beast. The great ape had run from its cage and barreled toward him, a predator ready to snatch up its prey—but then it had stopped, peering at this man with a leopard's head suspiciously. Why wasn't he moving? Why didn't he run like all the others? Guin's seeming lack of fear was too much for the ape to comprehend, so it stood there, glaring at him with eyes full of fiery rage, and beat its arms against its chest and howled.

Guin did not move, but deep within his leopard mask, his

eyes narrowed and brightened with a yellow light as his thoughts became more like those of the noble creature whose face he wore than like those of a man. He stood perfectly still, waiting, letting the heat and the stench of the ape's breath wash over him.

Then, it came.

Without any warning, the ape reached out toward Guin with one of its long, hideously powerful arms. Had it grabbed him head-on, the fight would have been over then and there, but Guin was ready. At the exact moment the ape extended its hand, Guin ducked under its grasp, and moving as though he had done this a thousand times before, he rushed in to close the gap between himself and the great beast.

The ape's breath was now filled with rage and a burning eagerness for the fight. Its arms swung through the empty air where Guin had stood only a moment before; then it drew them back in a convulsive clutch, attempting to hug the leopard-man to its chest and there wring the life out of him. But Guin ducked under the massive arms again and seized the creature by its throat and side. Dropping low, he hurled the beast forward, smashing its head against the stone floor with a wet thud.

A murmur rose from where the Black Count and the knights were sitting, but the blow didn't seem to slow the ape. In a rage it rose and lunged again, arms reaching for the leopard head that bobbed and ducked maddeningly before it. But as the ape charged, Guin slid deftly to the side and behind it. Leaping onto its back, he wrapped his arms around the thick mat of fur above its shoulders, trying with all his strength to break its neck. The muscles that ran down his arms, like the roots of an ancient pine, rippled and bulged with the strain, but he only held on for a moment before the creature reached back, tore him loose, and tossed him to the floor.

Guin whirled in midair and landed on his feet, poised for action. Fighting something with several times the strength and weight of a strong man was no simple task, even for a warrior as powerful as Guin; already his sun-burnt shoulders heaved, and his muscular chest rose and fell with each gasping breath.

The ape, too, was wary. It had realized by now that this foe was different from the others—the frail humans the guards would throw to him now and again, playthings to be toyed with and then ripped apart. It pounded its chest and gave a guttural howl, then stared at this man that refused to give up like the others had. Its eyes filled with a violent, primitive hate.

"One!" rasped the count's voice, as he turned over the stopped hourglass.

The ape lunged again, but this time, Guin kept his distance, ducking to one side at the last moment. He had to play for time to recover his strength, and he was not blind to the fact that his earlier efforts hadn't slowed the beast at all. This aware-

ness did not take the form of conscious thought, however;
Guin did not distract himself with concern for his situation, or
ponder why it was that he was fighting the giant ape. He was like
a leopard now, a wild beast, trusting instincts alone, moving by
instinct alone.

The grey ape hesitated, and for a moment there was a
standoff between the two combatants, neither willing to make a
move.

"What are you doing?" spat the count, swiping up a nearby
water jug and throwing it out into the arena, where it smashed
just in between the ape and the leopard.

The sound of the jug breaking was the trigger the two beasts
were waiting for. The Gabul ape leapt forward. Guin dodged
aside, the ape's arm missing him by a hair's width, and tumbled
across the floor. When he regained his feet, the leopard-man
held a jagged piece of the broken water jug in his hand. A gasp
went up from the knights.

Guin crouched low, waiting for an opening, his hands
almost resting on the stone floor. The next time his enemy
lunged, Guin let its arms wrap around his head as he drove his
makeshift weapon directly into the ape's left eye.

The ape's howl shook the dungeon walls, but it did not let
go of Guin's head. The warrior clutched at the ape's fingers
with his left hand, struggling against what seemed like the grip

of a thousand men, while he gouged deeper with the shard in his right hand. He cut down into the ape's cheek and still the howling beast did not relent.

Guin felt himself being lifted off the floor. He kicked the ape's stomach as hard as he could, then kicked again, but still he could not escape from the iron grip that now threatened to crush his head like an overripe gourd.

The knights held their breath.

Now Guin began to growl, a wild snarling cry that lingered in the air. If his head were not protected by the tough leopard mask, it would surely have been crushed soon. The skin of his neck was red from the exertion as he flailed around, repeatedly striking the ape's face with the weapon in his right hand.

When one of his blind thrusts sent the sharp stone shard into the ape's forehead right above its other eye, the ape finally relaxed its grip. Guin delivered one last sharp kick to the beast's abdomen before being tossed aside like a rag doll. The ape put a grimy hand to its face, and its cries of rage echoed through the dungeon.

The leopard warrior, battle-broken, lay on his side, motionless on the floor. Even the ape's great strength had not managed to rip off that leopard head, but it did look slightly warped as he lay there, blood oozing from his broad shoulders and chest where the ape's claws had raked him. He struggled, trying to stand, but after ineffectually kicking the air once, twice, three times, he gave an anguished growl and curled up into a ball, cradling his head in his hands.

The Black Count gasped, and leaned forward, the hourglass long since forgotten.

The great ape had lost one eye, and the vision in its other eye was blurred by the blood streaming from the cut directly above it. It stomped its feet and pounded its chest, its incredible rage still growing. It bellowed once, waving its arms around in search of the one who had caused it so much pain. Finding nothing but empty air, it bellowed again, and then again.

"Quickly, to your feet, leopard-man!" one of the knights shouted a warning to Guin, but the leopard-headed warrior did not rise. His badly punished head was swimming in a haze of pain; his eyes saw nothing but darkness before him. The stone shard slid from his hand, and he moaned.

The ape's hand fell upon the broken fragment from the water jug, and it growled and put the shard in its mouth, crushing it to dust in its fangs. Its rage was a black thing, a hissing hot fury born from ancient darkness.

Then its searching hand brushed the fallen body of the warrior!

"Look out!" one of the knights shouted. Another knight stood and quickly drew his longsword.

"Leopard-man! On your right!" he shouted, and hurled the sword out into the hall where it clattered on the stone.

Guin opened his pain-clenched eyes as the weapon was thrown. He darted out his hand, and like the leopard-god Cirenos who, it is said, caught a bolt of lightning, he grabbed the hilt of the longsword with a firm grip before it had stopped sliding.

The ape howled, and pounced upon him—but the longsword in Guin's right hand met the beast's charge with such force that the creature was stopped in its tracks, its chest split with a great red gash. The ape's howl of pain filled the ears of all in the chamber numb.

With all the agility of a leopard, Guin sprang to his feet. Slick with the hot blood that sprayed from the foul ape's chest, he moved in closer, thrusting and slashing again and again with the longsword.

Still, the monstrous creature stood, a testament to its bestial vitality. Its blind rage still boiling, the ape of Gabul grabbed the leopard-man by his battle-scarred shoulders, trying to rip the very meat from his bones.

Guin thrust the sword in deeper. When the ape did not let go, he swung the blade up and lopped off the fingers of one of its hands.

The ape's grip on him slowly relaxed, and he jumped back

and away as the beast staggered and fell. The knights could see giant, purple claw marks welling up on his shoulders, like an evil brand from the hand of Doal himself, and their eyes widened with terror.

Like a cruel but cautious predator, Guin thrust his sword into the ape's neck, finishing the thing off. Then he wavered and collapsed to the floor in exhaustion, still holding the longsword in his hand. His body was barely recognizable, spattered with gore and streaked with wicked claw wounds.

Just then, the hourglass ran out for the second time.

"Fool!" Guin faintly heard the Black Count Vanon shouting before everything slid away into exhausted darkness.

"Fool! Your interference has ruined my test! You—the knave who threw his sword to the leopard-man—step forward!"

"My lord, if I may," said a captain, who had been on the verge of throwing a sword to Guin himself. "The leopard-man has well displayed his ability to fight, as you can see! Indeed, I am forced to admit that there are none in my squad that could fell a grey ape in two turns of the clock, longsword or no!"

"Fools! Foolsss!" The count was furious.

"Has he not proven his worth, my lord?"

"Nothing has been proven except your ignorance! I never intended to throw him a blade. What would be the point? Any

Mongauli champion worth his armor could take down the capital of Torus itself single-handed, if he had but a longsword! I wanted to see him rip the grey ape apart with his bare hands!"

"But, but that's—" The captain's voice faltered. He blanched and stepped back. The count came limping over and pointed at the dejected culprit, who was pushed forward by the knights around him.

"Take off this fool's armor. Take it off, now! I will punish him myself. And take away the leopard-man. Lock him in his cell again, and feed him. We will have to wait until the barbarian traders come with another beast before we can test his prowess more fully...but wait. I have a better idea," the count said, clapping his hands together as though he was applauding his own devilish idea. He turned to the captain. "You, give this kind-hearted fool your sword, and lower him into the arena. If he can defeat the leopard-man, I'll make him captain of the third squad in your place!"

The count chuckled. "Quickly, off with his armor, give him a sword, lower him down the stairs!"

The captain protested. "My lord Count! That leopard warrior took a grey ape of Gabul down in two turns! How can Orro of Torus hope to fight him and live?"

"Who said anything about him living, my dear captain?" replied the count in a voice as cold as the stones of the dungeon floor. "The leopard-man is wounded and weakened. Should our insubordinate knight succeed in even scratching the leopard-man, I will overlook his foolish act. Now, down the stairs!"

The Black Count pressed a button on the wall and the stone stair lowered down into the arena once again.

It was only a moment, but that was all Guin needed. The hunched, blood-spattered, seemingly unconscious warrior sprang to his feet. The knights' cries of astonishment were still in their throats when, clutching his longsword drenched in the grey ape's blood, Guin raced up the stair and leapt over the partition, charging straight for the accursed lord of the keep himself!

Before the Black Count could so much as lift a hand, the leopard warrior's sword was at his throat. Guin grabbed the diseased noble's cloak in his left hand and gave a shout of victory. The knights took a step back.

"Clear a path, if you value your keep-lord's life!" howled Guin.

"It speaks!" said one of the knights in utter astonishment.

"Clear a path, now, or I slice open this rotting hunk of flesh right here."

The knights feared their lord's dark plague enough that they were uncomfortable even breathing the air around him; but they had sworn their swords to the glory and honor of

Mongaul, of which even he was a symbol. "Knight of Gohra" was synonymous with bravery and loyalty. For a moment, they hesitated, looking at one another. Then as Guin pushed the count forward at sword-point, they hurriedly stepped back, uncertain of their duty and frightened both by Guin and by their own lord's disease.

"Hands off your hilts!" barked Guin. "Orro of Torus, was it? I will not forget your kindness." The leopard warrior looked around. "Give me the keys to the white tower, and take me back to the place where I was imprisoned."

Guin stood at full height, his longsword held at the keep-lord's throat, his golden head barely clearing the low stone ceiling. There was something commanding about the half-man, half-beast—a majestic aura mingled with savage pride. The Gohran knights sensed this, and followed his orders with only slight hesitation.

But Guin's human shield, the count, invisible within his plates of iron, had other ideas about the situation. As he walked in front of Guin's blade, he began to laugh in a grating voice like that of a ghoul, sending shivers up the backs of all around him.

"What's so funny, pus-bag?" snarled Guin.

The count laughed louder. "I see now. He can wield a man's sword, but he has the brain of a leopard! Too bad, that. If he were smarter, he wouldn't have chosen me as his shield."

Guin stopped. "You are the lord of Stafolos Keep, no?"

"That I am," answered the count, sounding quite happy with himself. "I am the lord of Stafolos Keep, yet I am also the accursed Black Count of Mongaul—a fact which you seem to have forgotten. So take your sword, plunge it into my chest, please! Or would you cut my throat, instead? There is no plate there, just a thin iron mask that keeps the wind from touching my skin, and my disease from spreading. The moment that sword in your hand cut through my mask, the plague would spread to all of you here, and you would join me in living decay!"

Guin froze, then released his grip on the cloak, hurriedly stepping away.

The count laughed again. "Why wait for the sword to cut my mask? I could just take it off right now and feel the cool air of the dungeons on my accursed flesh..." Vanon raised his iron-gauntleted hand slowly toward his mask. A ripple of panic spread through the knights. Shouting and scrambling, they rushed in a mob toward the exit passage, each vying to be the first out of the room.

Their captain did not move to escape, but even he fumbled for his pendant of Janos, then raised his hands above his head and shouted, "Mercy, your Excellency, please!"

Slowly the count turned to face the leopard warrior. Guin stood as though stunned; the longsword fell from his hand, and he made no motion to resist when the keep-lord shouted, "Seize him, and lock him up back in the tower! Follow my orders without hesitation from now on, and you will be spared my...my fate. This I promise."

There was a great clanging of armor as the knights rushed forward and drew their swords. Each placed the point of the blade toward his left breast, the hilt toward the count, in the Gohran manner of oath swearing. Then they struggled to be the first to seize the leopard-headed warrior. Two of them wrapped Guin's powerful arms several times round with thick leather cords.

The leopard-man did not resist. He had looked within Vanon's mask, and now his fiery yellow eyes were dim and unfocused in shock, as if he had seen something so horrible that his mind could not grasp the reality of it. Grim and bewildered, he allowed himself to be bound, his sword taken away.

"Excellent," said the count, waving his hand toward the knights. "And I trust none of you will henceforth forget whom you serve. Now...I am tired. My diseased body yearns for my darkened chambers. Take this man to the white tower, wash him, bind his wounds, bring him food, and let him rest. I will test him again, and then, perhaps I will take him with me to the arena when I go to the capital to deliver those brats of Parros to his Excellency, the Archduke." The Black Count paused, catching his breath. "Now, be gone. I leave the punishment of the insubordinate who marred my test in your capable hands, captain."

Then the count's voice changed, as though he could no longer hold back his rage, and he screamed for the prisoner and the knight to be taken from his sight at once. Hurriedly, the knights moved to follow his orders, and it occurred to Guin that it was fear, deep and piercing fear, rather than the glory of Gohra or the loyalty of the Mongauli, that kept order in Stafolos Keep.

Quietly the little troop returned along the dark corridors. The hour was late, and the knights' footfalls sounded heavy on the floor, splashing in the shallow pools of water that collected in the cracks and hollows in the floor. The longswords at their sides clanged against their armor as they made their way up the passage, helmets drooping, looking down at their feet.

"Hey, watch out," came a low voice from Guin's left side.

Guin stood at least a head above the tallest man there, and he was about to strike a particularly low part of the ceiling with his head when the warning came. He shot a glance to his side, and saw there a knight with no sword in his scabbard. From beneath the black helmet a youthful face peered out with the characteristic blue eyes of a Mongauli. It was Orro of Torus, the one who had thrown his sword during the fight against the grey ape.

Seeing Guin nod thanks, the young knight spoke again, an almost reverent look on his face.

"Yer a great warrior." His voice was low, so as not to be overheard by the captain at the head of the line. "I couldna just watch ye die out there, I'd 'ave no right ta wear me sword if I did," he said, nodding in fervent agreement with himself. "I tell ye, I'm right glad I didna 'ave ta fight ye, either. Mighty glad, I was."

The captain glanced back and Orro fell silent. Guin kept quiet, and the party finally finished its ascent of the last stone stair and emerged into the courtyard. An overwhelming sense of relief flooded into the leopard warrior with each deep breath of fresh nighttime air.

Still Guin said nothing. He walked forward mechanically, but his keen eyes were clouded—they hid the spark of a terrible notion that had just begun to take root in his mind. But no one knew what suspicions were racing through that round, golden pelted head but he; and so the party continued across the courtyard and into the white tower, and climbed up the stair once again, their footfalls echoing off the narrow walls.

—— 2 ——

For the second time since he had arrived in the keep, Guin heard the sound of the heavy cell door being barred behind him.

He stood with his shoulders hunched, his back to the door, and studied the cell. The young prince of Parros had been facing away, curled up under some furs on one of the beds, but the sound of the door opening had woken him. Guin was back! The boy had been on the verge of shouting, but had held his tongue when he saw the black knights in the doorway. Stepping down from the bed, he ran over and simply clung to the warrior instead.

With the boy's slender arms wrapped around his waist, Guin nodded gently as if to say things were going to be all right. He was tired—incredibly tired—from fighting, and weak with hunger, but it did his heart good to merely stand there and stroke the boy's hair, soft like silvery silk.

"You came back," whispered Remus, watching the door close behind him. "I was so worried—I thought you'd be killed."

"Worry not, child. I live," Guin laughed. "It takes a great deal more to kill one as stubborn as I. Now...I need food, and wine, if there is any."

"Yes, Guin." The boy rushed over to the table, bringing back the remains of his dinner and the wine jug, and watched as the leopard-headed warrior launched into the cold meat, sticking his finger into the grain mash and noisily chewing as much as he could fit in his mouth. Clearly he had adapted to eating through his mask.

After a while he noticed the boy's intent look. "What is it?" Guin asked. "Your sister, is it? Don't worry about her, she can take care of herself."

"No, that's not—" Remus broke off what he was saying and went over to the cell door to make sure no guards were listening. He came back and whispered in the leopard ear. "The man next door..."

"The 'Crimson Mercenary,' was it?" asked Guin, between draughts from the jug of wine. It was mulsum, a drink of fermented honey popular in the lands of Gohra, and he found it quite good. "What about him?"

"Well..."

Guin looked over at the wall between them and the neighboring cell. The loose stone had been returned to its place, closing the small window between the rooms.

"I fell asleep...a pretty deep sleep, I guess, and...well, when I woke—" Speaking slowly, as though afraid of a scolding when he was finished, Remus recounted what had happened while Guin was away. After the warrior had left, Istavan had asked Remus for his bed sheets and spent a good while fashioning a rope, but then he had lain on his bench and begun to snore.

Remus had watched him for a while. Growing up in the beautiful palaces of Parros, with no one but stuffy royalty and obsequious servants to play with, the boy had never encountered anyone like the wild-spirited Istavan, and the mercenary had sparked his curiosity. Remus had tried to talk to him a few times, eventually giving up when there was no reply but the soldier's snoring. Then he had sat down to wait for Guin. He was just starting to nod off, when suddenly he heard movement in the next room.

"Great Jarn!" came a whispered curse, followed by the sounds of someone quietly moving the furniture next door. Remus jumped from his chair and put his eye to the hole in the wall. The "Crimson Mercenary" had lowered his newly made rope through a large hole in the outer wall, and was starting to crawl through the opening!

"Wait, you!" shouted Remus, sticking his face through the small gap between their rooms. "That rope ladder belongs to me, too! Where are you going? Guin isn't even back yet! Wait, hey, wait!"

"Quiet, boy!" said Istavan, glaring at him. "Shut your foolish mouth or the guards will hear you!" The mercenary continued working his way down the rope, not bothering to wait for Remus's reply, and soon he disappeared in the darkness of the night outside.

"So he tricked me!" said Remus, finishing his story. "He said he was going to escape with us!"

Guin's laugh was almost a howl. "So, Istavan has escaped! Don't worry, he has his own destiny to follow. There is no way we could get through that little hole into his room to use that rope ladder anyway." Guin turned to look at the opening. "Besides, he had no intention of escaping with us in the first place. He might have brought me along, for my sword, but children are a burden he would not have accepted. I guessed he would do as much—he seemed clever enough."

"But he tricked me into giving him my sheets!" Remus was furious.

Guin laughed harder. "You are too trusting, my little prince," he said, turning back to look at the boy. "You gave your faith too easily, and you were betrayed—but you cannot let something like that anger you, if you should ever want people to call you their king. I tell you not to worry, even though Istavan has left me in the same fix. I'll think of a way to get you and your sister out of this keep unharmed, but let's let the mercenary walk his own path. Meanwhile—I am very tired. Let us leave escape for later. Now, I must sleep."

Guin closed his eyes and sprawled out on the floor where he'd been sitting. Remus walked quietly away so as not to disturb him, and was making himself comfortable in the corner of the room when Guin's eyes suddenly opened.

"Your sister, Rinda—she is a seer? I would do anything to have her divine the truth behind something very strange I saw just before coming here."

"What did you see?" Remus replied irritably. He didn't always like to be reminded of his sister's powers of sight—powers that he did not share.

Guin shook his head, as if trying to rid himself of an image burned into the back of his eyes, and rolled up in a sleeping fur.

"Your sister said she didn't want to enter this keep, that she could feel something in the air, that the fortress was doomed. I thought she was just talking about the count's disease. But down in the dungeon—after they made me fight a great ape of Gabul—I tried to escape; I took the keep lord as my shield and I...I saw something very strange."

"Something strange?"

"Yes." Guin sat up suddenly. With the fur still wrapped about him like a ragged pelt, he stared out into the darkness of the room. It was as if his shining eyes peered through the solid rock of the walls, searching the entirety of Stafolos Keep for something.

"Perhaps I should not say 'strange'—for all I saw was the lord of Stafolos Keep, the Black Count Vanon. Perhaps it was a trick of my eyes...yes, that is what I want your sister to tell me: that I was seeing things, that it was the cold of the dungeon that chilled me to the bone."

Guin shivered. "You do not understand; you were not there. I had the count at sword-point. I was standing this close to him, when my body began to shake like I had come down with a fever. I tried to stop the trembling, but it was no use. My legs, my arms, every part of me shook like a young bird in a nest of vipers. It was as if I was hanging above the mouth of hell by a thin thread, and I looked down into the abyss and saw...nothing."

Guin kept talking, now more to himself than to the boy. "The count was laughing like a crazed magpie... He threatened to take off his mask right there and let his rotting plague ride on the wind to all of us, and the chill feeling grew strong, terribly strong. I was the closest to him, closer than all of the knights, so

I saw something they could not, or rather...I saw *nothing* better than they could."

"That makes no—" began Remus, but Guin cut him off, his fingers moving unconsciously to make the sign of Janos in the air.

"What I mean is, when that diseased creature began to pull down his mask, I saw where it joined the armor below, and I saw nothing."

"Nothing?"

"Not one thing under that mask but empty space."

Remus swallowed.

"It's true," said Guin. "I couldn't believe my eyes. I dropped my longsword, so shocked I was. My eyes can see baltos roosting in the tops of Roodwood trees, or a grass snake winding through a thicket, but when I looked behind the Black Count's mask, where there should have been at least a withered head, there was nothing. Had there been anything—a shadow like the night sky, with twinkling stars—I would not have been so shocked. But what I saw through that crack was an abyss like that of the lands of Doal—it was the abyss of hell itself.

"It was only a tiny crack, but the tepid wind blowing from it raised bumps on my skin, and the smell of rot grew until I could bear it no longer."

Guin's eyes closed in recollection. "I want to know what he

is," he said, after a moment. "I want to know what this Black Count Vanon really is."

The warrior and the little boy looked at each other in silence. The currents of their thoughts drifted unbidden to the soldier from Valachia, the mercenary Istavan, and his seeming conviction that all their lives were in danger if they did not escape the keep before night's end.

Mark my words: you'll have every accursed stone in the place coming down on your head.

"Guin…" said Remus in a shaky whisper. "What's going to happen to us?"

"I don't know." Guin's voice was firmer than before. "But I know we cannot sit here with our fingers crossed to see what fate brings us. Whatever might await us outside, we need to get out of this tower and out of this keep. Child, if it comes to a choice between the fear that seems to live within these very walls and the zombies of the Roodwood, I will take the zombies!"

"But, what about Rinda?"

"She is coming with us. I'll find a way." Guin tilted the jug to drain the last drops of honey wine before curling up once again. "And as for this Mongauli apparition…I don't know what to think, so I won't. What will come to be, will be. No point wasting energy worrying about it now." With these words, the warrior closed his eyes and quickly fell asleep.

Hunched in the corner, Remus watched his leopard-headed companion. A dark, uneasy image had risen in his mind, vague but terrible, and it was not until long after Guin had gone to sleep that the image finally began to lose its form and fade.

It did not seem that this would be a night of quiet rest for anyone in the keep.

Just moments after Remus had finally settled down to sleep, there came the loud clanging sound of men in armor running up the stone stairs of the tower, followed by a creak as the bar on the prisoners' door was lifted. The door opened, and a torch was thrust into the room.

"Two in here—the leopard-man and the prince."

Guin turned and sat up, asking angrily whether captives of the Mongauli were not even allowed to sleep.

"This one's fine." The tall knight who stood in the doorway waved on the men who accompanied him, then turned back to Guin.

"Didn't you hear the guards shouting? Seems one of you captives got it into his mind to go for a swim in the Kes," he explained. "He's a fool that'd jump into the dark waters of the Kes, but we've got a bunch of them dirty Sem in here, and *they'd* probably be right at home in there, they would. So we've got to see which one of you jumped."

"How do you know it was a prisoner?" asked Guin, a smile in his voice. "Maybe it was a Gohran soldier, sick of guarding this place every day."

"No Gohran is so weak," said the knight proudly, "and the sentry said the jumper climbed from this tower."

"How can anyone be so sure," asked Guin, "when demons make their nests right here in this keep of Stafolos?"

Even in the dim torchlight, Guin could see the color drain from the knight's face. Cursing, the man put his hand on the hilt of his longsword and made to step into the room, when he was arrested by a shout from the next room over.

"Here it is! The prisoner jumped from here! He's dug a hole in the wall, he has! You, jailer! Who was in here?"

"A mercenary from Valachia—said he talked back to his Excellency the Count."

"He'll have a hard time getting across the Kes...though Valachia *is* near the sea and maybe he thinks he's a swimmer. Send an order down—get guards out there with torches, shine them on the surface of the water until we find the corpse."

There was more clanging and footfalls outside as the scattered guards came clamoring back down the stairs.

"Freak!" the knight spat and walked out, swinging the door shut behind him.

"I hit a sore spot, it seems. They know there's something amiss here in the keep all right." Guin sounded pleased. "I wonder if Istavan made it down in one piece. He seems like a man you could kill a hundred times before he died—but swimming in the Kes, and at night..."

"Guin?" Remus's quiet voice came from where he sat hunched in the corner. Guin looked up. "Is it really true that you lost your memory? You really don't know who you are? Guin, sometimes, it seems like—"

"I don't understand it myself," Guin replied. "Sometimes I say things before I even realize I knew them. I don't even know what I know, and what I don't. But...I do not know who I am...or who I was. That much is true."

"I was thinking, when they took you away to fight in the dungeons," said Remus. "Rinda and I, we've only been with you for a couple of days now, but somehow it seems so much longer—like we've known you forever. You told me not to trust too easily, but I never doubted you once. I thought, maybe, could you be someone we know?"

Guin chuckled. "A warrior serving the royal house of Parros?" He thought for a while, then shook his head. "I do not think so. In my mind, I can see the great Kes, and the barbarian lands beyond—I know these places. But Gohra, Parros, all the lands of the Middle Country, these are like a hole in my memory. No, it is like I never knew of them in the first place, like someone planted in my head all the knowledge I might need to live in the Marches, but left the rest a blank sheet. They dropped me here to find my way...to where?"

"You mean you don't remember Parros? The Crystal Palace? Or the Mongauli capital of Torus, surely you must remember that! Yulania? Kumn?"

"Nothing." Guin held his head for a moment, then growled. "There is an aching in my mind... This word, 'Aurra,' is like a pounding hammer, it's all I can hear."

"Whatever could—" began Remus, but then he let out a cry and pointed at the window. "Guin! Look! The sky outside, it's red! Is it morning already?"

"No. They've placed torches along the keep walls—searching the river for the Crimson Mercenary, no doubt."

"Oh..." said Remus, thinking again. The torchlight reflecting off the river surface was enough to paint the entire cell with flickering red light. "So, Guin, maybe you came from the territories to the north, or the lands to the south. No one really knows what's down there..."

"Neither do I."

"I don't think there's any land in the Marches that could train a warrior like you, though."

"Who I really am is not that important right now," Guin

replied brusquely. "Let's worry about that once we're out of this place. Now—sleep, child, even if just for a little while. Though it may be hard with all this light, I admit."

"What's that noise?" asked Remus suddenly. "Can't you hear that? Like many men talking all at once."

"The black knights searching for Istavan, no doubt. They've led out some horses from the stables and are sweeping the landing in the back."

"I...yes, I suppose that's it."

Remus seemed troubled. Guin chuckled. Compared to his sister, Rinda Farseer, the little princess of Parros, Remus was easily scared, always jumping at shadows.

Yet this time Guin was wrong. He was mistaken about the cause of Remus's unease, just as he was blind to the true potential that still lay dormant in the young boy—or mostly dormant. Remus certainly did not have the powers of prediction that his sister Rinda had, but he *was* her twin brother, and they shared two halves of the same soul. What never occurred to Guin was that Remus's trembling, his fear and his unease, might be precisely the kind that the warrior himself had experienced earlier, in the dungeon.

Guin turned irritably toward the wall, away from the brightness of the window, and attempted once again to give his wearied body the sleep for which it ached. The red torchlight spilled into the room and over the round shape of his leopard head, painting a strange shadow on the wall. Remus sat with his arms around his knees, weary and weak, but unable to sleep. He sat staring at the warrior.

"Guin...Guin..." he whispered, but there was no answer.

What's wrong with me? thought Remus. He could only come up with two answers: either he was completely without courage—as cowardly as a little girl—or else it was that his twin sister, with whom he shared his soul, was also lying awake up in her tower room.

He had never tried to feel for his sister over a distance—there had never been a need, for they had never been more than a room apart before now—but, twins that they were, with the blood of the priests of Janos running in their family line, a little white magic between them would hardly have been surprising. Perhaps Remus's senses were telling him something. What if Rinda was in danger? A sudden, pressing unease came over him, and he hugged himself more tightly and closed his eyes, focusing every thought on his sister.

"Rinda...Rinda...Rinda..."

Nothing happened. After a while, he sighed and stood up. Taking care not to wake the sleeping Guin, he moved a chair quietly to the window; then, climbing atop it, he peered out of the small opening at the world outside.

A cool night breeze hit his face. Instead of the dark, sleeping forest and the mountains in the distance, all he could see was the blazing red of dozens of torches, burning the night sky, and reflecting off the grim black walls of the keep.

Then a thought came to Remus. All those torches were surely keeping the search parties safe from the terrors of the Marches at night when fiends ran rampant, but wouldn't those same red flames cast so many shadows that the searchers' flesh-and-blood quarry might find it far easier to hide? A shiver ran down Remus's spine, though he couldn't have said exactly why. He didn't care whether Istavan was caught or not, did he?

The night air was filled with the constant commotion of the search parties and a pervasive feeling of unrest. A thin hint of purple outlining the edges of the distant mountains told of the approaching dawn. Remus put his hands on the stone of the wall and listened to the whinnying of the horses, the constant barking of orders, and the swishing of leaves as riders beat through the brush, and he thought that he wouldn't mind it if dawn decided to come just a little early today. The sun brought a thousand blessings—it was the protector of mankind. The golden orb's rays would brush away the malignant wings of night where Doal ruled; its penetrating light would reveal all things. The fiends that hid in the night, the ill omens, the danger, all succumbed to the dawn light—and even if Remus and

Guin and Rinda were still trapped in this accursed keep come
morning, it would be enough that they had lived through the
night. The dawn would teach them to look at all of the portents
and the night-worries, and laugh.

"It was just like this," whispered Remus, remembering,
"when the crystal city fell in flames, when the blood flowed and
the screams and terror came in the night. It was just like
tonight." Though no one was listening, Remus put his soft
cheek against the cool stone of the wall and ruminated on his
life—until these last few bewildering days, a long peace spent in
the shining light of the crystal city. *Will Rinda and I ever see the crystal
spires of Parros again? Will we ever see anything beautiful again?*

The watch lights of the sentries burned red, pushing back
the night, and the moon hid its bluish-white face behind a thin
veil of clouds. Heeding a sudden impulse, Remus stood up
straight on the chair and looked outside again.

There was something out there in the night, something
great and terrible. Remus felt his eyes drawn upward until they
lit upon the source of his fear.

"The black tower!"

It stood close to the keep walls, directly across from
Remus's cell halfway up the white tower. Even from his narrow
window, he could see that the black tower had neither windows
nor any openings for light at all, as though it were designed to

hold an unspeakable malaise festering deep within its impure darkness.

Remus's fingers unconsciously made the sign of Janos to ward off demons, and the boy quickly jumped down from the chair and ran across the room to sit hunched against the far wall. But the sight of the black tower lit by the watch fires was burned into his mind like a wound, a horror forged from the misfortune and terror of the night itself, that could find him and haunt him even through the wall.

Remus moved quietly towards Guin, careful not to wake him. His feeling of terror grew until it was almost more than he could bear; his breathing came in gasps, and he put his fist to his mouth and bit his knuckles. The back of his head burned and went numb, and he curled up in a ball, somehow knowing that they would not make it through the night unscathed; that something would go catastrophically wrong before the break of day. Istavan had sensed it with his animal instincts—that's why he had jumped into the black flow of the Kes like a rat fleeing a sinking ship. Remus wanted to jump, too. Dangerous though they might be, the waters of the Kes were far preferable to sitting here at the mercy of the fear that gnawed at his stomach.

And then Jarn quietly gave the little wheel of his fate-loom another turn.

And Remus heard it.

Through the pre-dawn darkness, over the faint sounds of the search below, came a girl's shrill voice—not to his ears it seemed, but directly to his heart.

"Stay away, demon! You touch me once and I'll bite my own tongue off! Help! Somebody! Remus! Remus! GUIN!"

There was no question: it was Rinda, and she was in trouble. Remus jumped to his feet, shouting at the top of his voice to be let out. Guin stood up, startled, staring at the boy.

Somewhere down below, the keep bell began to ring.

—— 3 ——

Rinda Farseer, the little princess of Parros, sat with the Sem wildling girl Suni in their tiny, windowless tower room, and waited. Separated from Remus and Guin, locked up with a stranger that did not speak her language, Rinda, if she were any ordinary child, would surely have been frightened to the point of tears by now.

But Rinda was an unusually strong-willed little girl, accustomed to facing the future. The potent flame of hope burned in her breast, and she had faith in her destiny. And so she had managed to completely forget her current troubles, and sat at ease with her hands on her lap, engrossed in her attempts to communicate with the even smaller girl sitting next to her.

"Wall," said Rinda, to which the wildling, barely three feet high, mouthed back, a little dubiously: "Wa-ll."

"Hand."

"Ikkuku, neeni, reedohra, eemi!" said Suni, chattering a

stream of words in her high voice.

"How am I supposed to understand when you say so many words all at once?" Rinda complained. Suni had quickly tired of being the proper student—or perhaps she was upset that Rinda, in typical royal fashion, had showed a great deal of enthusiasm for teaching Suni the language of Parros, but had made no attempt to learn Suni's tongue. Rinda soon despaired of the lessons. For a moment the two girls glared at each other, exasperated—then both broke into wails of laughter.

"I wish I had the Tongue of the Magi! Then I could speak any language I wanted to without all this fuss," Rinda exclaimed. Suni sat down at her feet, looking up with undisguised curiosity at her pearl-white skin, platinum blond hair, and tall, slender frame.

It seemed that the first impromptu language lesson had ended in failure, so Rinda changed tactics to the more direct approach of body language.

"Where," said Rinda slowly, pointing at Suni, "did you come from?" She pointed vaguely beyond the walls of their cell.

Suni tilted her head inquisitively, uneven locks of hair falling across her face, and then began to chatter and wave her hands. After numerous attempts, Rinda finally understood that Suni and a number of other Sem had been found by some of the keep knights as they were standing on a small sandbank in the middle of the Kes. Crossbow shots had killed several of them on the spot, while the knights had tied the rest of them in a line and dragged them away to the keep. As to why Suni and the other Sem had been in the river in the first place, Rinda could only assume that they were following some barbaric custom and hunting whatever nastinesses lived in the black waters that flowed through the wildlands.

Suni began to wave her arms again, this time seeming to indicate that others of her kind had been captured in this way by the knights many times before.

"You're the first Sem I've ever met, Suni," said Rinda, "so I don't know everything about you, but I'm pretty sure that those lands beyond the Kes are what we call the real Marches, where all sorts of dark happenings go on, and the only god is Doal, who is evil incarnate! Is it not so?"

Suni gave Rinda a bewildered look, shaking her head.

"The Gohrans are our enemies, too," continued Rinda, evidently not caring if she was understood. "They invaded Parros, and crushed the crystal city under their boots, ripping the silken curtains from our walls with their barbarous hands! There's no way you could know this, Suni, so I'll tell you. We— myself and my brother Remus, the heir to the throne of Parros—we stood there, holding on to each other for dear life as the black knights, the blue knights, and the red knights of

Gohra cut down the palace guards. Then...then they slew our father, King Aldross—he was a peaceful scholar, and high priest of Janos! We saw them all fall and drown in a sea of blood.

"Then Boganne, who had been our wet nurse, and Minister Riya came running up," Rinda continued without pause. "And they told us that now, we were Parros's last hope...last hope, Suni! Remus and I ran through the halls of the Crystal Palace—everywhere it was full of smoke—and then we came to a place we had always been forbidden to enter—the Spire of Janos!

"Boganne and Riya were in such a hurry, they kept rushing us, I remember, until we came to the Crystal Throne there underneath the spire. Then Riya reached out his hand just as the red knights came into the room, and one of them stuck his sword into Boganne's chest, shouting 'I've got them, the head of the prince of Parros is mine,' and I grabbed onto Remus and we were falling—

"And then, I know you're not going to believe me, Suni, but we were falling, and everything was dark, and I could hear Minister Riya shouting, 'The grid has gone mad! Pity, great Jarn, pity on us!' but he sounded so far away, and—"

Rinda stopped to catch her breath. "When we came to," she continued at last, "Remus and I were lying on our stomachs in the underbrush near the Roodspring! Count Vanon said it was the work of black magic, but to tell you the truth, I don't know what happened... I don't know how Remus and I found ourselves running for our lives through the smoky halls of the Crystal Palace one moment, and out in the Marches—in the lands of Gohra—the next!

"Not that this made our lives easier in the least, Suni! Why, Remus and I had no idea where we were, even that we were in the Marches—we spent two whole nights with only prickly vasya bushes for a bed. We ate vasya berries and licked dew off the grass. It was only because we overheard some black knights passing nearby that we found out we were in the Roodwood Marches, the outskirts of the Mongauli archduke's domain, and as close to the spirit-lands as we'd ever care to be. We found out that the black knights were riders on patrol from Stafolos Keep.

"We were lucky, really," Rinda admitted. "To survive two whole nights in the Roodwood—and then just when it seemed the black knights had caught us, that's when Guin appeared. A leopard-headed warrior, straight out of legend—he only remembered his name, and a single word...'Aurra.' Nothing else—"

Rinda's mouth snapped shut.

A sudden change had come over Suni's face. She abruptly stood up, wavering unsteadily, and held her hands out in front of her almost as though she were begging for mercy. Then she screamed.

"Aurra, Aurra! Aurra!"

"What is it?" Rinda exclaimed, bending over the little girl. "You know that word, 'Aurra'? Tell me! What—or who—is 'Aurra'? Do you know him? Do you know Guin?"

"Alphetto, reeni, imeeyaru!" Suni screamed. Rinda could not understand the language of the Sem, but the way these words were spoken made their meaning clear: "Alphetto-god, save me!"

"Suni, really!" Rinda said sternly, but then she saw how frightened the little Sem girl was and bit her lip. If this word "Aurra" alone was enough to strike fear into a Sem, what could its terrible meaning be? What fate could have left Guin with his memory robbed of all but that one word? Whatever it was, it seemed to hint at some dark history from the lost time when the warrior had become entrapped in his leopard mask, leaving him looking as though the goddess Irana had cursed him in her wrath.

"Suni! Please tell me—what is 'Aurra'?" Rinda grabbed the terrified girl by the shoulder and shook her. "Was Aurra the one who left Guin to die in the Roodwood with that leopard mask on? Please, tell me, what do you know about Guin?"

"Imeeya! Imeeya!" shouted the little wildling, fearfully raising both her hands before her and twisting them together in the air.

This was all a little too much for Rinda. Her patience with Suni was running out. She shook her again, harder—when suddenly the little girl's eyes went wide and her body became rigid in Rinda's grasp. Her eyes grew white with terror as she stared at something over Rinda's shoulder.

"What—" Rinda noticed Suni's expression and stopped shaking her. She had all but forgotten the ominous feeling of danger that had surrounded her since she entered the keep, but now it all came rushing back. "What is it…Suni?" Rinda's voice was low and trembling. The fear in the Sem's eyes was so intense Rinda's heart crept up in her throat and she froze, not wanting to look back over her shoulder at whatever it was Suni was watching.

But soon the fear of having her unprotected back facing whatever was behind her overcame her fearful immobility. Biting into her lower lip with her pearly teeth, she let Suni go—though she could still feel the little girl's furry hands grabbing on to her for dear life—and then, slowly, she turned to face the wall.

Where was the wall?

A massive tapestry—its design impossible to see in the gloom of the chamber—hung behind her, and in the still air of the room it began to flutter, then blow away from an ever-widening gap where the wall had once been!

Rinda grasped Suni's little hand tightly in her own, unconsciously holding her breath. She could feel the girl's violent shivering travel up her own arm. Rinda stared at the widening darkness; an unwholesome moldy stench crept into her nostrils.

"Who...Who's there?" the princess asked, her voice rasping with fear, then tightening into a loud squeak.

For a second, she thought that the wall had opened into hell itself—that they were standing at the entrance to Doal's audience chamber. The reeking stench increased, wafted on an unnatural wind. It brushed against Rinda's cheeks, seeming almost conscious, alive; she had to close her mouth to keep from retching. She made the sign of Janos and a moan came unbidden to her throat.

Suddenly, a figure emerged from the black hole where the wall had been.

At first, it was a vague, glimmering outline that seemed fashioned out of the fabric of the darkness itself, but Rinda's sharp eyes saw a human shape—at least, it might have been human—with a hood over its head and a long black cape mantling its body down to its feet. It was the cape that made the figure so hard to distinguish from the blackness behind it.

When the cloaked shape moved again, Rinda saw a face hidden deep in the hood, covered in hastily wrapped white bandages. A chill ran through her.

The Black Count!

Slowly, the cloaked form raised an unsteady hand, loose bandage ends fluttering down as it beckoned to them with malformed fingers.

"Alphetto," moaned Suni, too frightened to scream.

The cold stone walls that confined them seemed nearer and nearer now, while the darkness of the one terrible exit yawned deeper and deeper. The apparition stepped closer, and the girls stepped back, keeping the distance between them until their backs were flat against the farthest wall. Not once did they take their eyes off the slow advance of the black horror before them.

An oppressive odor of decay now mingled with the stench of mold and seemed to clutch at the very breath in their lungs. The cloaked figure shuffled forward with what seemed like an incredible effort, holding out its hands as though it were blind in the dim light of the room. Rinda felt the bile rise in her throat again, and she shook with terrified loathing; but even as she did, a small, alert portion of her mind noticed that, although the shambling thing stood right in the path of the wind that blew against her face, the hem of its long cloak didn't so much as ruffle in the air.

"Hiiih!" screamed Suni, finally breaking out of the spell that had held her frozen to the wall.

"Vanon..." the words choked in Rinda's throat. She wet her lips. "Count Vanon—if you are truly Count Vanon..."

Rinda tried to wring the words out of her unwilling throat, but they froze in her mouth.

The cloaked figure lurched to the side, then raised its arms as though it were praying—or begging for salvation—and suddenly, lunged for them!

"Aaahh!"

This time it was Rinda's turn to scream. The cloaked figure shifted, and the bandages on its face slipped, revealing the most horrible, rotting black...*gruel*, thought Rinda. She could hardly have called it the remains of a man. It only took a heartbeat for all her sense of pride and seer's bravery to abandon her, leaving nothing but a scared young girl where once had stood the little princess of Parros.

"H-Help!" Rinda shouted, clinging to Suni, their backs pressed to the stone wall, both of them screaming with hardly a pause for breath. The moving corpse, the impure monstrosity of rotting flesh, was terrifying beyond words, and the thought that this thing was human—a Mongauli lord, and master of Stafolos Keep—only made it worse. Yet the eye that stared at them through the gap in the bandages, half-covered by rotting, jet-black flesh, gleamed with an undoubtedly mortal need...it wanted something of them. But what?

"Hiiih! Hiiiii! Hiiiiii!" screamed Suni. Rinda shook her head, desperately trying to clear away the worsening stench of decay. The monstrosity closed the distance between them, its collapsed eye shining with unspeakable thirst and a mad craving. The bandages slipped off of the sloughing flesh of its arm, baring the bony hand of a corpse that clutched at the shoulders of the trembling girls.

Suni went limp in Rinda arms, leaving the young princess cradling the little girl. Rinda's violet eyes were frozen on the apparition. She very much wanted to fall unconscious, too—anything that would free her from the sight of this horrible living corpse—but she knew that if she did, the thing would be able to do whatever it wished with her, and that fear kept her from slipping away. She simply stood frozen, and stared.

The broken, shapeless arms waved up and down, twice, three times, as if trying to give some signal. Then they came down, almost touching Rinda's shoulder. Rinda saw a face more grotesque than any skull peering out through the ichor-stained bandages, and the powerful stench assaulted her senses with renewed force, draining all the strength from her limbs. But at the moment the long bony fingers made to touch her soft skin, Rinda's surging fear broke the spell that held her motionless, and she gave a cry that seemed to rip right out through her throat.

"Stay away, demon! You touch me once and I'll bite my own tongue off! Help! Somebody! Remus! Remus! GUIN!"

Then she screwed her eyes shut, and fell down atop Suni on the floor, covering her face with both hands so that she need not see the monster that approached her now like some grotesque parody of a lover in the throes of passion seeking to claim a kiss.

Then she heard it—Remus's voice ringing in her head as clearly as her cry had rung in his. "Rinda! Where are you? I'm coming to save you! Rinda? Rinda!"

"Here, Remus! Up here! Help!" she shouted in reply. Even with her hands held firmly over her eyes, she could see the decaying claw reaching for her, the disease spreading to her skin where it touched her, causing her flesh to rot away... Rinda sobbed.

Then she heard a bell clanging. No, it sounded like many bells, all over the keep, ringing with a sudden fury and insistence that could only mean one thing—danger—danger far worse than an escaped prisoner or a wildfire in the Roodwood. The bells seemed to ring everywhere, pounding on Rinda's ears without pause. Now she could neither hear nor see, so she slowly lifted her hands from her eyes.

"It's gone!"

The black-cloaked apparition that should have been looming over her, its diseased body smothering hers, was gone—vanished into thin air as if it really had been a ghost.

Gone, too, was the opening in the wall behind the tapestry, which now swung slowly back and forth on its hooks. Rinda leapt to her feet and ran over to it, sweeping the heavy cloth to one side with her hand. Behind was only a flat, unbroken wall of heavy stone.

"But...but that's impossible! I saw it open!" Rinda put her hand to her mouth in shock, her voice barely audible over the *kang kang kang* of the bells.

"I know that foul stench was not my imagination! And that creature, that horrible creature! B-But how is it that we are safe, Suni? Wasn't its disease supposed to ride on the slightest breeze? We were so close, surely we should have fallen sick by now—but we're fine! You saw it, too, didn't you, Suni?" Rinda looked around in utter bewilderment, but there was nothing but the stone walls on every side, and the pealing of the bells that seemed alternately to come closer and to draw farther away, like waves on the shore: *kang kang kang!*

In between the ringing, she could hear faint sounds of commotion down in the keep grounds: swords clanging, the whinnying of horses, then screaming and shouting. Surely something was wrong down there! Then a voice rose clear above the pandemonium—

"The Sem are attacking!"

Rinda jumped forward as though she had springs in her

legs. But there was nowhere to run, and, beyond wringing her hands together nervously, there was little she could do—she was still a prisoner in the tower.

The sound of the watchtower bell stopped suddenly, as though one of the Sem's poison arrows had caught the bell-ringer in his throat and killed him before he could raise his mallet for one last ring. Rinda kept rubbing her hands together, crying out in frustration. Then she ran to where Suni lay like a discarded rag on the floor and took her up into her arms, rocking her and calling her name, anything to wake her up. Whatever was happening down there, she certainly did not want to face it alone.

—— 4 ——

Had a lone demon been looking down on Stafolos Keep for the last few hours, perhaps from the nearest of the mountain peaks, he surely would have laughed at the twisted paths of fate the mortal folk beneath him were walking.

The keep stood on a rise of land surrounded by two forests—the Taloswood and the Roodwood—with the Kes River at its back. It was known as a dangerous post for a soldier, for the territory over which the keep kept watch was unstable at best, with the peoples of the Middle Country in constant conflict with the barbarians of the Marches. Thus the keep was built to take advantage of what natural defenses there were.

If any attackers should come by land through the forest, they would be forced to ascend by a long narrow road that wound up to the top of the hill. The road was too narrow for two to walk abreast, and so the enemy would have to come single-file, while the guards at the top could roll rocks and fire shot upon them at their leisure. Behind the keep, a sharp cliff fell down to the Kes River, so steep that only the occasional water snake or lizard could climb it—the perfect defense against an attack from the rear.

The nearest tribes of Sem barbarians made their home in the wildlands beyond the black line of the Kes. As long as they stayed on their side of the river, and the keep inhabitants kept a close watch out for raiding parties, there was little danger—but tonight, after the commotion of recent events, the guards were not watching where they should have been.

Had that demon on his mountaintop been observing Stafolos Keep since the beginning of the night, and had he eyes that could see both inside and outside its cold stone walls, he would have seen countless small figures slipping into the black flow of the Kes, sliding down the black riverbank that looked out on the wildlands of Nospherus, and swimming soundlessly toward the other side, throughout the night.

The tiny figures looked much like monkeys; judged by their height they could scarcely be more than children or wood-sprites. Yet they braved the dark waters where few would venture, where many horrible things were known to lurk—demonfish, water snakes, and worse. Unlike their foes, the Sem were friends of the river; they had tamed its terrors and knew its secrets. One after another, the small shadows sank into the great stream until only their black heads were showing above its surface.

The Sem had tried many times in the past to attack the keep and drive back the human soldiers of the Middle Country that had violated their lands, yet every attempt had ended in failure, for the Mongauli had been able to catch the barbarian forces divided on either side of the river. With the Kes blocking their route of escape, the Sem who were stuck on the near side were soon outnumbered by the keep guards and slaughtered.

But this time, the small dark forms crossing the river in wave after wave late into the night came in far greater numbers than had ever been seen this close to the keep. They crossed without a sound, upriver and downriver, emerging from the current and running into the trees until they filled every inch of the Taloswood and those parts of the Roodwood that had not been destroyed by the fire. And still they kept coming.

It was just before dawn, and the larger part of the Sem forces had succeeded in crossing the river, when suddenly torches lit all around the rise and a great commotion began inside the keep walls.

The Sem chieftains grew anxious. Orders flew down the ranks, and high-pitched chattering arose from all sides. Then the scouts at the very front of the lines heard voices coming from the keep.

"Someone's jumped from the tower into the Kes!"

"The Valachian's escaped!"

More orders passed down the lines, and the chattering ceased. Those that were under the cliff beneath the fortress pressed their bodies as flat as they could against the rocks, and those in the woods lay low and quiet, and they waited for the keep to quiet down again.

But the keep did not go back to sleep. Guards rushed to the battlements and set torches on every wall facing the Kes. Certainly Jarn, the wizened fate-weaver, with his hundred ears and single never-sleeping eye, was in a fickle and mischievous mood tonight. The torches cast their combined light down the cliff, making the surface of the Kes glitter as if the sun itself shone upon it, and the Sem at the cliff's foot grew greasy with the sweat of fear, flattening themselves to the ground as the venomous lizard does in the midday heat.

Yet Jarn, for his own secret reasons, did not forsake the Sem this night. Had the keep guards merely placed torches by the river, a sharp-eyed sentry would surely have seen the invaders before long—but the soldiers had also built huge watch fires in the outer courtyard to stave off the foredawn cold. The light from the larger blazes was enough to turn the sky red, and fill the keep grounds with the brightness of midday, blinding the eyes of the keep watchers.

"Prepare the boats! We will search the river at dawn!" shouted a captain amidst the troops that huddled around the fires.

"Ach, that runaway's fish food by now, *he* is," came a soldier's voice.

"The count's orders are to find his body, and that is what we will do!" the captain replied.

The sky above the keep glowed ruddy orange, deepening the darkness of the woods and the black river, which concealed great numbers of Sem from the watchers at the keep. The unexpected alarm had given the chieftains pause, but the dark of night was their greatest ally, and they knew that if they held their attack until dawn, the advantage in battle would shift in the keep's favor. Quickly the wildling leaders gathered and conversed in low voices, then spread back out among their troops, giving orders to the warriors of each of the tribes.

At last the leader of all the tribes raised his hand and snapped his horsetail whip in the cool night air. Before the crack had finished echoing off the cliff side, the Sem nearest to the keep had begun to nimbly climb the fortress walls that faced the Kes, while those hiding in the forest quietly closed the distance between themselves and the battlements.

In the outer courtyard, flasks of wine and mead were passed around the watch fires as the men jested and slowly became

drunk. No rafts or boats would be sent out until dawn, they said
between bites of vasya fruit, their hands stained red from peel-
ing the rough skins—and why bother hurrying to find someone
who had jumped into the Kes? If not the rocks, then one of the
water spirits would make a floating corpse out of him soon
enough! Not one among them cared to go out into the Marches
at night, much less down the black waters of the Kes just to find
an escaped mercenary. Here, surrounded by the high keep
walls, they felt secure; warming their faces by the fires, drinking
from the flask as the mead was passed from hand to hand, they
let their watchfulness fade into drowsy contentment.

Suddenly one guard stood, his eyes wide open, looking
beyond the fires. He seemed about to shout something, but
before a sound escaped his lips he fell to the ground, scratching
at his throat. The startled soldier beside him moved to help,
lifting him from the ground, and saw that a tiny poison-coated
Sem arrow protruded from the dying man's neck.

The soldiers nearby hurriedly turned to face the outer wall,
only to see fur-covered shapes like monkeys springing out of the
darkness. Demon fangs jutted out of faces stained red with the
juice of the me'ea fruit, and a potent odor wafted off hairy bodies garbed in ragged wolf skins. A guard began to scream, but a
heavy stone axe caught him in the head, cracking his skull in two
and spraying its contents over the nearest of the watch fires.

For a moment the soldiers flew into chaos. The night was full of Sem, streaming over the keep walls, leaping down into the courtyard. The first wave of wildlings launched their arrows from atop the walls, felling scores of soldiers, then drew their stone axes and charged.

But the Gohran soldiers recovered quickly. They were awake and in armor, ready to hunt the escaped mercenary, and they had not left their swords by their beds. Battered out of their initial shock, they flew into a rage and drew their swords, slicing into the swarm of monkey-like fiends.

The Sem had the advantage of numbers and surprise, but their size was so inferior to that of the average foot soldier that they were forced to fight in groups against each single foe, like a crowd of mad children around a man. Each of the Gohran soldiers was confronted by at least half a dozen of the human monkeys leaping from every side.

In the midst of the battle, a lone black knight swung his broadsword from side to side, sweeping away the creatures in front of him, making his way to the bell tower and up its winding stair. Reaching the top, he stood tall, braving a hail of poisoned arrows, and began ringing the bell to warn the keep of the attack.

"Sem in the night! The keep is under attack!"

Kang, kang, kang, kang! The bell rang furiously as the knight yelled out the alarm—until a stone axe fell on his head and an arrow pierced his right eye. His body toppled off the tower and fell to the cobblestones below where the black knights were desperately trying to wrest control of the battle from the Sem. Forming a long line, they fought with their backs to the doors to the tower and the inner keep; but the Sem fought bravely too, breaking through the knights' defenses, surging toward the buildings. Each side pushed against the other, and the line of battle wavered, now out into the courtyard, now back toward the tower.

Out in the night, a cry of "Eeya eeya eeay!" rose from the leaders of the Sem lying in the woods, and they began to swarm along the narrow road up to the front of the keep. Those Gohran soldiers still on the outer wall barred the gate and raised the bridge at the top of the path, but with more than half of their number fighting for their lives in the courtyard, they were too few to take advantage of their position. What few arrows and rocks they could shoot down on their foes hardly seemed to make an impact on the massive numbers of Sem storming up the path.

Behind them in the outer courtyard, the tiny wildlings were slowly but surely pushing the keep defenders back. The soldiers there now fought with their backs up against the inner gates, slashing right and left at their small and agile foes; they began to realize that they would soon be overwhelmed by the numerous Sem, who swarmed both inside and outside the keep.

The captain of the fourth squad, plume streaming behind his black helm, saw five young knights, freshly arrived from Torus, fall with poison arrows stuck in their cheeks and eyes.

"Keep your heads down! Lower your faceplates, and look away from the outer walls!" the captain shouted, swinging his longsword to sweep the little demons off the battlement where they stood with arrows nocked. Just then, one of the wildling monkeys jumped down onto his back with stone axe raised. A nearby knight yelled a warning and pushed toward them. The Sem jumped clear and swung his axe to meet the approaching warrior, breaking the knight's black helm in two. The man fell to the ground and the Sem warrior scrambled for the wall, but the captain caught him before he reached it, swinging his longsword to cut the little fiend's head clear from its body.

The captain of the third squad, which was defending the inner gate, risked a look over at his brothers fighting under a hail of arrows by the keep walls. "We're as good as dead if we stay down here!" he shouted, and turned to a nearby knight. "You, guard this gate for just a second—I'm going to open it and run inside to get orders from the count—one second is all I need!"

"Yes, captain!" came the knight's reply, his voice strained with fear and excitement. The captain heard the youthful voice coming from under his helm and recognized Orro of Torus—the very soldier who had only just escaped execution in the dungeon arena earlier that day.

"On my count!" said the captain, slapping Orro on the shoulder and laughing grimly. "One...two...three!"

The captain turned his back to the fray and unlocked the inner gate. The Sem surged toward him, blocked at the last moment by Orro, who rushed in front of the opening and began to fight for his life. He was good: his sword was soon slick with blood, and with much jabbing and slashing he was able to hold them back from the open door. The captain disappeared into the dark and quiet of the inner keep, the door slamming behind him with a loud clang.

The Gohran soldiers resumed their formation and fought on, yet there seemed no end to their foes. The Sem were like the giant Nospherus, whose thousand heads grow back as soon as they are cut; no matter how many fell, more came to take their place. The Gohran soldiers battled fiercely, though the arrows and axes of their enemy were slowly taking their toll. It was this indomitable strength that had brought the knights of the small hinterlands country of Gohra from their humble beginnings in the Marches to the streets of the crystal city, to the seat of power of the Middle Country. Even when death was certain, they fought bravely for their country's pride and honor.

More and more arrows rained into the courtyard, and the bodies of the dead fell into the watch fires, sending eerily beautiful golden sparks dancing up into the sky. The screams and the war cries filled the soldiers' ears, and the light of the watch fires reflected off their blades—the fires were blazing hot now, flames searing the sky, their light revealing swarms of Sem flooding into the keep. The silhouettes of the towers floated above the men fighting for their lives like a strange mirage painted in flickering orange and gold. It looked as though the keep itself were broken and kneeling, sending a death-cry that echoed across the Marches.

"Aiee, eeya, aiee!"

The Sem chieftains raised their fists and gave a signal. A line of Sem archers let loose a volley of arrows streaming tails of fire, the missiles arcing high over the keep walls. Most clattered into the stones of the fortress and fell to the ground, but others struck wooden doors and posts, where they splattered and spread flame to the buildings. The chieftains gave the signal again, and another volley and then another of the fiery arrows flew over the heads of the embattled soldiers like a storm of shooting stars and disappeared into the inner keep.

Now the whole of the keep was lit with flames even brighter than those of the watch fires. This put the defenders at an even greater disadvantage, deepening the darkness beyond from which their attackers could fire with impunity. More Gohran soldiers fell with Sem arrows bristling from their necks.

"We're losing the main gate!"

The pathetic cry went up, and the soldiers strived to move toward the gate, but they were nearly buried in Sem on all sides, and they were soon forced to abandon their brothers to fight for their very lives. Their faces grew rigid with fatigue and their knees began to buckle under the weight of their armor; the Sem swarmed over them like ants on an elephant's leg, pulling them to the ground where their axes could reach the soldiers' unprotected throats.

Orro of Torus was still standing, fighting for his life with the other knights who defended the inner courtyard. He staggered—he had taken a light wound—but then he saw the sky in the east growing gradually lighter, beautiful rose and violet colors seeping into the clouds. Leaning on his broadsword as if it were a crutch, he shouted for joy.

"The sun is rising! Just a little longer and those Sem won't have a shadow to hide in!" He turned to encourage the guards fighting next to him. "We will win yet! We are the proud warriors of Mongaul!"

Orro raised his sword again and scowled. The Sem tribes had never before been so enraged that they would launch an attack of this scale on one of the borderland keeps—but now they were here indeed. The barbarians had penetrated even the inner bailey, and surely they would strike down and kill the Gohran soldiers one by one. Even if the soldiers' comrades in the keep at Alvon noticed the smoke rising from Stafolos and sent forces to their aid, it was a full three-day ride between the two strongpoints; the other keeps were even more distant. Orro shook his head. Right before his eyes, another black knight sank to the ground, his head split open.

Desperately Orro leapt forward, shouting as loud as he could.

"Reinforcements from Alvon Keep will be here soon! With the sun in the sky, we can win! Fight, brave warriors of Mongaul! Fight!"

He swung his sword to the right, taking the head off one of the Sem, then knocked aside an arrow with a backhanded stroke. *Where in hell is Lord Vanon now?* he wondered. *It's his keep that is under attack.* Surging forward, the young knight chased down a Sem covered in bright war paint who looked like he might be a chieftain; knocking away his foe's axe, he cut the wildling to the ground. If only the keep-lord were here; if only there were someone to lead them!

Orro paused in thought for only a split second, but at just that moment, a stone axe hit the back of his black helm hard, and multi-colored sparks shot through his eyes. He staggered and slowly sat down on the cobblestones of the courtyard, the broadsword falling from his loosened grasp. Immediately the battle surged over his fallen body, wildlings and knights clashing with increasing ferocity, until all of the Gohran soldiers guarding the inner gate were dead or too wounded to fight, crumpled beneath the axes of their foes.

An otherworldly howl of victory rose from the throats of the Sem. They rushed and danced over the bodies of the soldiers that lay in heaps on the ground, crushing them beneath their hairy feet as they rushed toward the inner gate. From the rear, a crowd of Sem brought up a large ram, and the gates flew inward with a crash.

"Yieee! Yieeeee! Yieee!"

"Yiee ieee!"

Screeching like monkeys, the wildlings jostled their hairy bodies together as they spilled into the dark chill of the inner keep. Orro's body lay wedged between those of comrades and foes alike, silent and still.

A great cheer rose from the Sem outside the main gates, followed by a tremendous crash of falling stones. The great gates had also fallen. Heedless of their fellows clustered inside, who were crushed when the wall collapsed, the next wave of attackers scrambled over the pile of stone and the corpses of their kin, screaming even more wildly than before as they rushed into the breached fortress.

Soon enough, the entirety of Stafolos Keep was filled with leaping, whelping little creatures. The Sem raised a queer cry and raced into the halls of the keep buildings, cutting down Gohran soldiers as they went. By now, half of the keep was in flames, and the parts that were not burning were buried in Sem. The shouts and orders of the soldiers ceased, turning to the faint groans and death cries of the wounded and dying. The flames crackled and spread, licking greedily with orange tongues at the two towers—one black, one white—that stood at the keep's very center.

Then dawn broke.

The sun came over the horizon, the child of Janos—a giant, crimson disk that lit the bloodstained stones as brightly as if the fires on the ground had leapt into the sky. High upon its crag in the middle of the dark forest, Stafolos Keep stood on the brink of perdition. The victory cries of the Sem and the crashing sounds of walls collapsing drowned the peaceful morning ballads of the woodland songbirds, while the fire spreading through the keep buildings shot up fingers of flame that wrote the words of apocalypse in the brightening violet sky above.

The clanging of the watchtower bell had long since faded; the watchtower itself was now engulfed in flame. Orro of Torus, lying with the corpses amidst discarded swords and broken arrows, was brought back to consciousness by the sensation of something wet running down his cheek. He wiped at it with his fingers—it was blood. Everything around him seemed vague and blurry, though he couldn't tell how much of this was due to the oily smoke that roiled everywhere, and how much was due to the pounding in his head. The courtyard was quiet, which meant that the hordes of wildlings must have already gone inside the keep buildings.

Orro stood up, wincing slightly, and began to walk unsteadily, using his sword as a cane. In every direction, the corpses of his comrades and the wildlings lay sprawled on the cobblestones. A hot breeze called up by the blaze swept through the courtyard, causing the cloaks of the dead to flutter. *These are the ruins of Stafolos Keep, pride of Gohra. One night is all it took for the strongpoint of the Marches defense to become this hell on earth.* Orro wept. He saw a Sem struggling to rise and stabbed it with the point of his broadsword. The knight's helm had fallen off, exposing his youthful, bloodstained face and blood-shot blue eyes. He started walking toward the white tower. The strength was slowly returning to his limbs. The fires on the main building of the keep were sweeping westward now, toward the white tower, from which the sounds of fierce fighting spilled out into the courtyard. Orro of Torus began to run.

A short while before, the third squad captain had entered the keep to bring word of the attack. He soon found himself running wildly down gloomy stone halls looking for his lord, or anyone who could tell him what he should do.

It felt to him as if the pandemonium of the courtyard outside had only been a passing dream, a fantasy brought on by fever and the stress of patrolling the Marches, so cool and silent were the inner halls of the keep. On account of the plague, few knights and fewer attendants ventured this far into the building unless their presence was required for scheduled audiences; on a regular day, hardly a living soul would be seen here. Now the building was utterly empty, and a sudden unease came over the captain as his footfalls echoed down the long corridors. It was as if he had somehow passed through a portal into an uninhabited world.

But when he stopped and listened, he could hear the faint sounds of the struggle through the walls: the screams and shouts, the clanging of blades and armor, the watch bell ringing out danger and the panicked neighing of the horses. He kept walking until the long, dark corridor finally came to an end, and he found himself at the foot of the black tower, his path blocked by two massive black barred doors.

The captain hesitated. Even the lowliest slave would surely have chosen death before passing through those doors, for beyond was Count Vanon—Mongaul's Black Count, alone with death, the smell of rot for his only company. The soldiers in the keep whispered that the count's body was rotting, slowly but surely, from the plague that would one day claim his life, and they cursed the fate that had placed them here, of all the many strongholds in the Marches, with a lord that seemed forsaken of Janos himself.

The third squad captain threw up his faceplate, his jaw set in a grim look of determination, and he threw back the heavy bar and opened the doors of death. A blast of the foulest air he had ever breathed hit his face, redolent of disease and rotting flesh. He grimaced and ignored it as best he could, shouting up the dark tower stair.

"My lord! Count Vanon!"

"What is it?" The reply came from so nearby that the man jumped back, startled, his eyes straining to see into the deep blackness inside the tower; but as far as he could tell, there was nothing there.

Black knight of Gohra though he was, the captain could not bring himself to step into the darkness where his diseased lord surely waited. He stood where he was and called out again.

"My lord, the worst has come to pass—the Sem are attacking, they are inside the keep!"

"I know," came the curt reply.

The captain felt a flash of anger—didn't Vanon care that his troops were outside in the courtyard now, being cut down with axes and felled by arrows? "My lord, they have come in great numbers. I doubt the keep will stand through the night."

The warrior spoke as calmly as he could, controlling his temper, remembering that he was speaking to an ill man. "The knights of the third are nearly finished, and the fifth has already fallen. The sixth squad now holds the gates, but if more attackers come, the gates will not stand. What would you have us do, sir…?"

"Let them fall then," the count said, the mocking tone in his voice clear. "Why should I care if the main gates fell? Let the monkeys take the keep, I have no need of it!"

"Lord Count!" the Third Captain sputtered in exasperation—his lord was mad, of that he was certain, and he sought for an argument that would convey the seriousness of the situation. "Why do you think the Sem have attacked in such large numbers? They are wild, yes, but since the year of the snake, there has been an unspoken treaty between us, and we have had peace…but now…this. It is because of *your* orders, Count—because you ordered us to take Sem hostages! It did not take long for the wildlings to realize what was happening to their brethren, and now they have come to rescue them and hurt us in turn. My lord Count, you are responsible for imprisoning their comrades in the tower, for..." The captain swallowed, and hardened his resolve. "For the disappearances. One by one, our prisoners have gone missing and the keep is filled with rumors that you are taking them! Why...what have you done to them?"

"I will tell you," whispered the count in a calm voice that came like cold fingers raking down the captain's spine. The man involuntarily took a step back.

"Captain, you are a faithful and brave warrior of Gohra. Leave the fate of the keep to the thread that Jarn has woven on his spinning wheel. I have other things to attend to."

"My lord!" The knight's voice was shrill. He took another step back. Before him, the darkness was slowly taking shape, revealing the form it had hidden until now. At last the Black Count of Mongaul—or rather, the thing that had been so named—appeared in the doorway, and the captain, rooted to the spot in fear, began to scream the name of the Dark One... And then the screaming stopped.

In the silence that followed, the viscous, foul-smelling darkness coiled back into the tower, and was gone.

Chapter Four

BEYOND THE BLACK RIVER

— I —

Stafolos Keep was in flames.

The battle was decided. Knights in black armor lay scattered in the courtyard and in the corridors, viscous inky smoke rising here and there among the bodies. The few remaining defenders had been pushed back towards the two towers in the center of the keep, fighting for their lives in a slow retreat. Outside, it was a brilliant day on the Marches. Other than the drifting cries of the Sem proclaiming the fall of the keep, there was nothing to disturb the calm of the wider landscape. The Kes flowed steadily on, a black ribbon under the sky which had gradually changed from a light violet to a soft blue as midday neared.

A short while earlier, before the defenders abandoned the courtyard, the keep had been filled with the clanging of swords and the cries of men, while a disturbance of another kind took place in the white tower where the prisoners were held.

In the inner court below the towers, the captains shouted

order after order, trying to stem the tide of Sem pouring through the main gate and bailey. The fourth squad captain had already fallen, shot with a poison arrow, and the captain of the sixth had disappeared beneath a swarming throng of the monkey-like invaders.

"To the towers! Protect our lord!" yelled the First Captain, a favorite of the count, and one of the few left in the courtyard still unwounded and with strength enough to shout. Gathering soldiers around him, he made a push for the two towers, arrows clanging off the iron back plate of his armor. He heard a great commotion ahead.

"The Sem are in the white tower!" a knight running ahead of him yelled.

The First Captain thought quickly—the white tower was mostly filled with captives of little account, but if the Sem took the white, they would have access to the black through the underground passage…and then there were the twins that his lord had worked so hard to find. "Never mind the other captives," he shouted. "Save the Pearls of Parros! Protect them at all costs!"

Gasping for breath, he turned to a soldier fighting nearby. "Sound your horn! The rest of the keep is lost, we must gather all who can still fight and move to defend the towers."

"Sir!" The soldier put his horn to his lips and blew a blast that trailed off when an arrow lodged in his neck, which was exposed for an instant as he lifted his head. Another soldier saw him fall clutching at his throat; jumping over, this other grabbed the horn and blew a stronger blast.

The First Captain heard the sound rising clear above the clamor of the fray, and he rested, his shoulders heaving with each breath. Leaning on his broadsword, he looked up at the beautiful blue sky. There they were: the gold savannah lion on a field of black—the Black Lion pendant of Gohra—streaming golden tassels; and beside it, the white and gold crest on purple, the flag of the Mongauli archduke, both fluttering proudly in the breeze as if to say that, should the keep fall beneath them, they would still fly. It was for this that the soldiers of the keep were laying down their lives. It was pride, it was pure beauty.

The captain's vision blurred and he lifted his sword. Shouting "For Mongaul!" he charged toward the white tower. All around him, men turned and followed the sound of the trumpet blast. They were running, fighting for their pride, the pride of Mongaul!

But the captain never reached the tower's gate. A wildling whip of cured wolf hide wrapped tight around his leg and sent him tumbling to the ground. In an instant, his large form disappeared beneath the furry bodies of the Sem, their stone axes falling on his back, a stone knife cutting his throat.

Up in the tower, the captives were banging on the walls of

their cells with whatever they could find, shouting to be let out. Not every room in the tower was filled with those who had received a death sentence from the bloodthirsty Black Count; most of the stone-walled chambers were empty, filled with silence and the occasional torq rat. But several did contain prisoners, and a few of those had windows to let in the light, from which the occupants had watched the battle spilling into the inner court, and the steady approach of the tendrils of fire that threatened to take the tower long before the invaders could claim it as theirs.

The corridors echoed with the sound of prisoners slapping the stone doors with the flats of their hands, benches and stools, and kicking and screaming to get the attention of the jailer. The clamoring was enough to drown out the battle outside.

"Jailer! Jailer!"

"What's going on out there?!"

"The wildlings have come! This keep's done for! We'll all be killed!"

"Let us out of here! Let us out! Give me a sword, I'll fight those monkeys! A Mongauli sword—I'll never run again!"

"For Janos' sake! If you keep us trapped in here those monkeys will peel our skins off, they will!"

"Jailer! Somebody! Everyone, the fire's on the wall! Ach, we'll burn in here! Let us out!"

The noise of fists beating on doors and the pitiful screams of one unlucky man who had been ignited by a flaming arrow that happened to fly through the small window in his cell mingled with shouting in every accent: Torusian, Valachian, a Marches drawl, even the booming tones of Kumn—each throat straining until raw.

The roar got louder and louder as the hunched jailer hobbled as fast as he could—which was painfully slow—up the dark stairway.

"Open my door! Let me out of here!" the voices yelled at every landing, pleading with him. The jailer walked up to each cell and slammed his key ring on the door, shouting back at the prisoners.

"No! No! Be silent! No talking! You will be freed when his Excellency has given orders, not before, not while I'm jailer here!"

"This is no time for displaying your loyalty, man! Leave us in here and you're sacrificing us to the Sem, you are!"

"Open up, now!"

"Silence!" the jailer roared. "I take who I'm supposed to take, and no more!"

Ignoring both insults and pleading, the jailer, followed by several knights, passed by most of the doors until he reached the room where Guin and Remus were being held.

The leopard-headed warrior and Prince Remus, son of his Holiness of Parros, the late Aldross the Third, were yelling and pounding on the door like all of the other prisoners. Remus seemed to have gone mad, screaming his sister's name over and over, and the door to their cell shook with the blows of Guin's powerful hamfists. The door itself was fashioned of a single slab of stone, and well-nigh unbreakable, but Guin's hands and giant body had nearly succeeded in battering it from its hinges.

The jailer barked for them to wait, his harsh Marches voice made harsher by exasperation. "I'll be letting you out now, so away from the door with you!"

"If you plan to take me to your rotting lord, I'll take my chances with the monkeys!" roared Guin, his voice sounding muffled through his mask and the thickness of the door. "Give me a sword! I have the right to defend myself against those sub-humans of Nospherus!"

"I've gotten no such orders," said the stooped jailer, chuckling. Sidling over, he lifted a key from the large iron loop at his belt, turned the lock, and then quickly stepped back as Guin, howling, burst out into the corridor.

"I have knights, beast-man!" screeched the jailer, quickly shuffling behind the black knights that had followed him. They stepped forward, the points of the long spears in their hands lightly tickling Guin's throat and chest. He roared a challenge at them, and from behind his powerful form the young prince of Parros cried out to the knights, trying to reason with them.

"Can't you hear the fighting outside? Guin can defeat your whole squad barehanded, but the wildlings will kill us all if we're fighting each other! Give Guin a sword!"

"The affairs of this keep are none of your concern, prisoner," the leader of the knights told him with an air of superiority. "You're to be brought to the safety of the black tower by the count's order."

"Safety? With that monster?" Guin scoffed. "There's no safety in that tower, and it's not the Sem I'm worried about."

"Who's the monster, freak?" The knight stabbed the tip of his spear through the skin on Guin's chest. Guin didn't flinch.

"You're coming with us!"

"No. I will not go near that Doal-spawned count of yours again."

"Why you..."

"Sir, downstairs!" one of the knights broke in hesitantly, stopping their enraged leader on the brink of beating Guin with the butt of his spear. " I think we may have a problem."

"The only problem is this presumptuous half-man!" snapped the leader, turning to the worried knight. "This keep will not fall to mere barbarian rabble," he said with evident pride. "We are the strongpoint of the Mongauli Marches defense! We've weathered many a siege and every time, our proud Mongauli swords have beat the enemy back! Besides, reinforcements from Alvon will be here short—"

Suddenly, he stopped, a curious look on his face. A second passed during which no one realized why he wasn't talking—why he was standing there like a giant comical puppet without a puppeteer.

The knight never got to finish his speech. Above the high and narrow bridge of his distinctively Mongauli nose, right between his eyes, a small arrow with two black feathers and a short black shaft stood sticking straight out like some strange fashion accessory, quivering from side to side. His eyes rolled up into his head and he fell back into the stone doorway, the metal of his armor crashing like thunder as he hit the floor.

"The wildlings!"

The knight who had sounded the warning stood spellbound at the sight of his fallen leader who, a moment before, had so loudly guaranteed their safety.

"Look out! Behind you!" shouted Remus, just as a stone axe came down on the unlucky Mongauli's head. The knight screamed, more in bewilderment than in pain, and joined his comrade on the floor. The next thing Remus knew, a dozen brown, furry creatures appeared out of nowhere, as though they were coming through the very stone of the walls, and began streaming over the fallen man, howling and chattering as they ran.

The hunchbacked jailer flailed his arms and turned to run,

ignoring a Sem arrow that stuck like a needle into the lump on his back. If he had been of regular height, it would surely have struck him in the neck, but hunchbacked as he was, he was barely taller than the Sem archer, and this had saved him. He dropped his key ring and made to run down the stairs, then stopped and cried out. An innumerable odorous mass of monkey-men was surging up the stairs, screaming in their alien tongue. They came like floodwater breaking through a dam, except that this flood flowed uphill.

"Save me! Save me!" the jailer cried out, flattening himself as best he could against the stone wall of the stairs, as though it could somehow swallow him up and protect him from the enraged horde. But the Sem did not mistake him for one of their own.

Shrieking like wicked birds, they fell upon the jailer. Pulling in his head like a turtle, he took three wounds to his back before one of the Sem jumped over him and stuck an axe deep in his forehead. The jailer toppled over without so much as a whimper, and began to roll down the stairs like a ball, bowling over several Sem before coming to a stop on the landing below. The wildlings rushed over him, their dirty bare feet scrambling over his body.

On the floor above, a fierce battle was underway. The knights who had quickly drawn their swords to resist the sudden attack were cutting down the Sem. They had the advantage of elevation, compounded by their natural advantage in height. They had been taken by surprise; but they knew the keep well, and the narrow stairs limited the number of Sem that could attack them at once. Fighting one on one, or two on one at most, the black knights were more than a match for the tiny Sem.

But the strength of the Sem was in their numbers. Even as their kin fell in a haze of blood, the monkey-men pressed on without hesitation, screaming "Aii! Aii!" as they charged over the bodies of the fallen. Behind them, a group of wildlings had snatched up the keys and were unlocking the prison doors, screeching wildly every time one of the great stone portals swung open. If a prisoner was inside, they would rush in with their axes and strike until nothing moved in the room, then move on to the next chamber. Some of the prisoners huddled under their beds, others picked up chairs and bravely fought these wildling fiends that dared to profane the domain of humanity. But the Sem dragged them out from under their beds, and swarmed around the ones that put up a fight like ants attacking a beetle until their prey succumbed.

Several of the rooms they opened were already blazing with fires set by arrows that had come in through the windows, and the stair corridor quickly became a hell on earth, filled with the crackling of the blaze, the screams of the dying prisoners, and the shrieking of the Sem, all mixed in the whorls of thick black smoke that grew thicker by the moment.

Remus, shaking, looked down upon the fray from further up the stairs, clutching at the sturdy wooden chair that was his only weapon. But Guin had not stood still for long. When the leader of the knights fell to the Sem arrow, the leopard-headed warrior had, after a second's hesitation, grabbed Remus and pushed him back behind the stone door of their cell.

"Stay there!" Guin barked. Then he grabbed the nearest thing he could find—the empty mulsum jug—and holding it up to ward off arrows, turned to go back out into the hall.

"Guin, no!" Remus screamed, but the warrior had spotted something: the fallen knight's sword was still in its scabbard at his side. Guin ducked through the door, stepping clear into the hall, and a ripple of astonishment ran through the Sem.

"Alphetto! ... Riyaad! Riyaad!" Their shouts rose above even their constant war cry, the tone in their voices making their meaning clear: "A leopard god! Mercy!" But then one of their leaders raised his hand and shouted something that seemed to bring them back to their senses, and lifting their axes they charged at the leopard-headed warrior.

Meanwhile, Guin had taken advantage of the wildlings' momentary hesitation to stoop and grab at the longsword lying on the floor by the fallen knight; but the hilt caught on the scabbard—it was stuck!

Guin growled deep in his throat, then pulled at the sword with all his strength—and a Sem archer, cackling like a crow, shot an arrow directly at him. Guin looked up.

The arrow hit him right between the eyebrows of his giant leopard head.

"NO!" Remus screamed and dropped his chair.

But it was the Sem archer who screamed next.

Ignoring the quivering black arrow, coated with deadly venom, that was sticking out of his forehead, Guin jerked the hilt of the sword back and forth until he had cut through the tangled scabbard; then he held up the freed blade with a satisfied growl. He swung the sword quickly to get a feel for its weight and balance, then rose calmly to his feet. He pulled the black arrow from his forehead with his left hand and casually chucked it back at the wildlings.

His aim was true. The arrow hummed like a dart as it flew unerringly to pierce the neck of the archer who had shot it. For a second, it seemed as though the Sem was immune to his own poison, but soon enough, the archer staggered, scratching at his throat, and fell motionless on the ground.

Fear shot like a bolt of lightning through the wildlings behind him, and cries of "Alphetto! Alphetto!" filled the narrow stair as the wildlings called on their god for mercy.

"Liirara, mul-straato!" shouted their leader, telling them not to be afraid and to continue their attack; but this time the Sem hesitated for more than a few moments before sending up another war cry.

Guin didn't wait for them to regroup. He was finally armed again. His warrior blood boiled, and he became a fighting machine, his longsword whining through the air as he cut through five of the monkey-men with a single sweep. Then he assumed a fighting stance with the sword held in front of him.

"Guin!"

Glancing around, the leopard warrior saw one of the monkey-men slipping past him into the open cell. Howling, Guin turned and ran into the room, cutting the wildling into two halves through the waist just as it was lifting its axe to strike Remus.

"On my back!" growled Guin. "They'll overwhelm us with their numbers if we stay here any longer. Whatever you do, hang tight!" He lifted the little prince up onto his massive back, then picked the Sem's stone axe up off the floor in his left hand, and brandishing the sword in his right, watched the fighting in the hall outside, waiting for an opening.

Here and there in the corridor and on the stairs, some knights and a handful of the more able prisoners were putting up a fight, but they were too far apart from each other. It was only a matter of time before the wildlings would win by virtue of sheer numbers—the defenders would be crushed beneath them, their strength and will to live exhausted.

Guin quickly took measure of the situation even as he slashed and parried to every side. He thought furiously, bringing all his animal craftiness and human resolve to bear. At last he shouted: "Everyone, to me! Fight alone and you will fall! We must fight together in one place to stop the Sem!"

"We'll never make it!" shouted one of the prisoners. "We cut and we cut and still they keep coming! 'Tis like fighting against the ocean, this!" he howled, then, as an axe caught him in the leg and he tumbled to the ground.

"Doal!" Guin spat, even as his sword flickered through the air, cutting another simian head from a furry body.

"Child!"

"Yes, Guin!"

"We cannot fight like this for long, and the fire is getting closer."

"What about Rinda, Guin?"

"I know. We must get to her somehow before the tower is buried in monkeys. If we keep moving upwards we'll be trapped..." Guin paused, panting. "But the Sem leave us little choice!"

"Behind you!" shouted Remus. A wildling warrior had snuck around behind Guin and leapt, improbably high, striking at his head.

"Ay!" Guin cut the creature out of the air, knocking its lifeless body against the wall.

"On my count!" he whispered, turning to Remus. "Grab my belt. On three, I will cut us a path to the stairs."

"Yes, Guin!"

"Ready? One...two...three!"

Guin lowered his head and thrust out sword and axe, lunging out into the sea of wildlings that had crowded into the stone corridor. Remus followed close behind him.

Guin's sword swung faster than the eye could follow, cutting into the Sem, sending up a crimson spray on both sides. An animal howl leaked out of his mouth, his eyes blazed gold, and he became a wild beast, his godlike physique coated in the blood of his enemies.

The wildlings wavered, then quickly retreated, avoiding the path of his charge. Guin cut his way to the stairs and began bounding up, taking three steps at a time with each great stride, the little prince scrambling behind him.

The floor above was already filled with the first Sem that had entered the tower. Guin kept swinging his sword, cutting down wildlings as he ran.

"Find your sister! Call her!" Guin shouted as his blade danced in the air.

Remus answered with a nod, and began to shout "Rinda!" up the crowded, smoky stair.

"Rinda! It's me! Rinda, where are you?"

There was no answer, so while Guin stopped on the first landing and fought to push back the pursuing horde, Remus ran to each of the doors, checking every cell. He soon returned, pale with worry.

"She's not here."

"Right. We go up." Guin gave the Sem one last sweep with his sword and headed up the stairs, this time sending Remus along in front of him. Few of the wildlings had made it up this far.

But Rinda was not on the next level either.

"Guin!"

"Up further, quickly!"

An ominous light shone in Guin's eyes. His head tilted to one side, as though he were considering something.

"Guin...?"

"Listen!" said Guin, holding up his hand to silence the boy. "Outside, in the courtyard—it's quiet. The only sounds of fighting are coming from inside this tower. If this means that the Sem have already taken the keep, and are now just cleaning up the remnants, even I don't stand much of a chance of escaping."

"Guin…"

The leopard-man growled. "Frown later, now we must run or be run over!"

Remus hurriedly turned and dashed up the stairs, which had become more narrow and steep.

"Guin, we're running out of stairs!"

"We're near the top, then."

The small landing they arrived at next was darker than the others in the tower, with a ceiling so low that Guin almost had to crouch. The stairs came to an end at a single prison door.

Hope filled Remus and he shouted, "Rinda! Rinda, are you there?!"

"Remus! In here!" came the immediate answer.

"Guin!" said Remus, turning to the warrior.

"Stand back!" roared Guin, and gave the door a shake. But it was made of a sturdy, single sheet of rock, and it hardly budged.

"Hrmm…"

Guin tried bashing down the door, but it soon became clear that his shoulder would break before the door gave in, and he gave up after a few tries.

Lifting his axe, he made to strike the door with it, but stopped with the axe in mid-air.

"Where did that jailer's key ring go, I wonder?"

"I saw it, Guin!" said Remus, suddenly remembering. "It fell in the hall outside our room, and then one of those wildlings kicked it and it fell into the water trough at the side of the hall. I bet it's still there!"

"Hoh hoh!" Guin chuckled and looked with satisfaction at the heir to the kingdom of Parros. "Not bad, my little prince. Now, I will go back down and get them, but first, I will make a barrier between this floor and the one below it to keep you safe. One of those doors should do nicely...."

He started down the stairs, then turned back to face the boy. "I do not think many Sem will make it past the barrier, but should they come..." He handed Remus the stone axe. "You are a boy, and will soon be a man. Your first lesson starts now. If they come, fight."

"Right, Guin!"

"Good." Guin clapped his hand on the boy's slender shoulder, and raised his bloodstained sword. "Protect your sister."

"Guin...be careful!"

"Do not worry, I..." he began, the yellow eyes shining out of his giant tawny mask with a sudden understanding. "It is not my fate to die in this place. Nor is it yours." His voice sounded almost gentle. Then, before Remus even had time to let those words sink in, the leopard-headed warrior was off like a whirlwind down the stairs.

When he reached the floor below, Guin yanked one of the open doors off its hinges, lodging it across the opening to the stairs going up. Satisfied with his makeshift barrier, he raised his sword and charged down to face the wildlings, who were just now arriving from below.

The stairway filled once again with the howls of the Sem and the sounds of fighting. The noise drifted up through the barrier to where Remus stood on the darkened upper landing, clutching his stone axe in sweaty hands, his back flat against the cruel stone door that separated him from his sister. The boy was praying under his breath: *Don't die, Guin...don't die!*

2

Guin swung his sword swiftly to right and left, sweeping down the stone stairs like a black and gold tornado, cutting down a never-ending stream of wildlings on both sides as he ran. He showed no signs of tiring. "Out of my way, wildling monkeys!" he yelled, his sword flickering and slashing, leaving tumbled mountains of corpses in his wake. His blade moved like lightning, dealing death with accurate blows—he was like the blood-soaked war god Ruah come down to earth.

As the leopard-man battled, he noted grimly to himself that the wildlings did fight bravely. It was almost as though the pre-human brains in those fur-covered skulls lacked the portions responsible for fear and self-preservation, so recklessly did they charge forward over the fallen bodies of their kin. He had little time to spend in observation, however, for they gave him little pause. A feline demon, he raged down the stair, not slowing until he reached the door to the cell chamber he thought he had left for good.

Oddly, the wildlings seemed to decrease in number as he went further down. Perhaps the main force had gone after other prey, leaving this tower to the group fighting Guin. The Sem had already abandoned this level—there were no keep forces here left to fight. Bodies—some Sem, some black knights, and a few prisoners—lay where they had fallen in the corridors and cell chambers. The cell doors stood ajar, some still swinging eerily. Yet Guin still had to deal with a new group of Sem who now ran up from below to face him, as well as the wildlings who were coming down after him from above.

Still, the odd quiet of the lower chambers puzzled him; and from outside...nothing. He could hear no sounds of the battle that had raged so furiously in the courtyard below.

So the keep has fallen.

Guin growled, and increased his pace. He had reached the place where Remus had said he would find the keys...and there, in the small open trough running against the wall that served as plumbing in the tower, he saw a metallic gleam. But he had no time to reach out for it, because at just that moment the Sem who had pursued him from the upper levels arrived. They fell on him ferociously, a dozen or two strong, and it was all he could do to keep them back with his sword.

If the final blow had been dealt to the keep, and the last of the defenders had fallen, the wildlings' next move would surely be to set fire to whatever buildings remained. Guin didn't have much time left.

He knocked the stone axe from one of the monkey-men's hands with a skillful blow, then cut another small Sem from shoulder to gut on the backswing; then, with his back pressed against the wall, he fought, waiting for an opportunity to reach down and grab the key ring.

But the relentless onslaught gave him no pause—more drastic measures were needed if he was ever going to get those keys. Gritting his teeth, he turned his eyes from the swarm of fiends attacking him; then in one motion he hunched down and snatched the keys from the trough with a swipe of his left hand.

All this he did in the flicker of an eye—but in turning he had left his broad back exposed and undefended for that one moment. The Sem closest to him had hesitated for a tenth of a second, thinking that perhaps this was some sort of tactic, a trap to lure them in—but when they saw his eyes on the keys, they came in quickly with axes held high.

By that time, Guin was already starting to stand, but he had thrown away the advantage he had held before, and he looked up to see an axe whistling through the air, coming right at his head. Rapidly he blocked the blow with his sword, but the blade was slick with the blood of more than a hundred wildlings, and

instead of bouncing off it, the axe slid along the steel, scraping Guin's upper arm on its way down. Guin's sword slipped out of his hand, bouncing off the wall with a clang.

"Look out—here!" came an unexpected cry from somewhere behind the Sem. It was followed by a new sword, arcing over the mass of furry heads towards the leopard-man, who snatched it out of the air with ease. Shifting his grip, he swung in a semi-circle, mowing down the wildlings closest to him just in time. Had the sword not come to him just then, a stone knife would surely have bitten into Guin's left shoulder.

What a fine weapon he had received! The blade wasn't even notched, and Guin cut into his foes with renewed strength, all the while searching for the one who had come to his rescue. There he was—fighting for his life against a group of wildlings who had broken off from attacking Guin to assail this newest combatant.

Guin's mask was expressionless as always, but a satisfied laugh spilled out from underneath the rigid leopard jaw. The one who had thrown him the sword was none other than Orro, the young soldier from Torus.

"That is twice you've saved me, Orro of Torus!" roared Guin as he merrily dispatched a never-ending stream of wildlings.

Orro had his hands full with his group of Sem, but he shot

a glance over at Guin and curled his lips into a smile. Still, he had taken many wounds, and he did not know whether he would be able to stop that big Sem that was—where did it go? His sword cut through empty space. During the fraction of a second that Orro's attention had been turned to Guin, the wildling had slipped behind him and was now leaping, its axe raised above its head in mid-strike.

Orro sensed the attack and turned to meet it—a mistake, for the blade took him squarely in the forehead. His head was bare—he had already lost his helm down in the courtyard—and the axe cut deep. Orro staggered and spun around twice like a top, blood streaming from the cut, before falling heavily to the ground.

"Orro!"

Guin shouted the youth's name and ran towards him, sending Sem flying through the air with every swing of his weapon. At last, the barbarous stream had abated—there were only a few left now. Lifting Orro from the ground with one hand, Guin turned on the remaining wildlings with his sword in the other, finishing them off in a couple of blows. Then he gently shook the young knight.

"Orro of Torus, don't die on me!"

"I'm sorry..." gasped the youth in reply. "Ye...ye'd best get out of 'ere, while ye can. They'll be back with more, they will...

E-Even if ye are the war-god Ruah, ye canna fight 'em all yer-self. There's more of 'em than there are ghouls in the Roodwood…" Orro's voice trailed off.

"Don't talk," said Guin. He had laid down his sword and begun looking about for a piece of cloth or anything else that might be used to bind Orro's wound. The skin of the knight's forehead was cleanly split, and it seemed that the axe had cracked his skull. Orro weakly shook his head.

"Flee, leopard-man. I did what I came 'ere ta do, and…on me way in I saw black smoke rising from the white tower. Wouldn't do for a warrior like yerself ta b-be burning up in a foul place like this, eh? It…was good seein' ye fight."

"Don't talk, Orro. You've saved me twice, now it's my turn to return the favor."

"All's I did was give ye me sword. Y-You were the one what used it. You saved yerself…leopard-man? Wh-Where are ye?"

"Right here." Guin waved his hand in front of Orro's face. The youth's eyes were staring into nothing, unfocused. "You want water?"

"No, I…ahh! Stafolos! Was she not beautiful? And now…what an 'orrible fate ta befall 'er… A captain fell, right before me eyes, 'e did, and Leede from back 'ome, and Eke—a good friend 'e was—all of them killed by those monkeys. Ach, curse the 'undred ears of that bloody geezer Jarn and the unjust fate he weaves." Orro coughed. "I was supposed ta finish me tour here this spring, I was. Out of the Marches and back ta the beautiful streets of Torus..."

Orro's throat made a rattling sound, and he fell silent. Guin held the youth still in his arms and watched the color of life slowly drain from his face.

Then the youth twitched. "Ach...it hurts. Aaah..."

"Do you want anything?"

"No...not anymore, not..."

"Have you family in Torus?"

"Well, I..."

Orro slowly licked his lips, then spoke with some difficulty. "Listen. Should ye ever need 'elp in Torus, ye go find Godaro at the *Smoke and Pipe* in the markets. That's me father. 'E's a good man, and 'e'll want ta know 'ow 'is son died—fighting them Sem barbarians...a warrior's death..."

"Godaro of Torus. I understand." Guin took Orro's hand. It was already cold, the grip weak. "You did good by me, Orro."

Orro's wounded face twisted into a smile. He opened his mouth. "Ye...yer a great warrior, leopard-man," he whispered with the last of his strength. "If I'd not thrown ye me sword, I'd be no true war...warrior of Mongaul."

His voice broke off, and Orro of Torus was gone.

Guin solemnly picked up his sword and laid the young

knight's body on the stone floor, swearing, "The next dozen heads I take are for you." The expressionless leopard mask tilted slightly forward.

Then Guin looked up from his crouch. His nose had caught a whiff of smoke, and he heard the sound of another commotion nearby. Sem reinforcements in the tower!

"Iyee! Yee!"

"Aiyy! Aiyy!"

Faintly Guin could hear the strange cries coming up the stairs. He leapt to his feet, and leaving Orro's body behind, he sprang up the stairs once again. In a single breath he had reached the stone door that he had placed as a barricade. As he pushed it aside, he heard Remus's voice choked with tears of relief.

"Oh, Guin!" Remus ran down to the foot of the last stair. "Guin, Guin, I thought they killed you..."

"What's this?" said Guin, by way of reply. "It looks like you handled yourself in a manner befitting a prince!" He noted the five or so dead wildlings in the space beyond the barrier. "I had thought you a meek little dove, but I may have been hasty in my judgement."

Remus's cheeks glowed with pride. Guin brought out the keys and began trying each of them in turn in the door.

"That's the one!" he growled at last as the lock emitted a soft click. The solid stone door swung open and Rinda came flying out.

"Remus!"

"Rinda! Rinda!"

The last hours had been the loneliest the twins had ever known—the Pearls of Parros separated for the first time in their lives. Now they hugged each other tight as though they would let nothing keep them apart again; they cried and kissed each other's cheeks. They stopped only when Guin gave a sharp snort, his eyes flashing as he peered into the room behind Rinda.

A shrill scream came from the darkness. Rinda spun away from her brother and ran into the chamber, grabbing Guin's raised sword arm with both hands.

"Wait, Guin, stop! That's my friend! Suni's harmless, she's good! Stop!"

"Your friend?"

"The Black Count captured her—that's why the other Sem are here, they've come to save her! Once they see that she's okay they'll let us go, I know it!"

"I think not!" howled Guin. "Children, behind me! They're coming up the stairs!"

"Suni will talk to them!"

"Behind me I said, little fool princess!" he barked. "Doal be burned! They're bringing fire up with them. Those little monkeys can swing down from here on vines, but we'll be cooked to a crisp in this tower, or—they come!"

The first bunch of wildlings rounded the last corner of the stairwell, reaching the top floor of the tower. Suni ran out of the room, going forward to meet them. But when she saw the first few Sem, she gave a shrill cry and leapt back behind Guin and the twins.

"Suni, what's wrong?"

Suni was chattering rapidly in her high voice.

"What is it? Your friends are here to save you! Talk to them, Suni! Tell them we're friends!"

"That won't help," said Guin. "She says they aren't from the Raku tribe she belongs to. These Sem are her tribe's enemies, the Karoi."

"Guin!" Rinda raised her hand to her mouth, which was gaping in surprise. "You understand her language!"

"So it seems...but that's of little use to us now. It seems our luck has just run out. This girl cannot help us; and below we have Sem chieftains who are unlikely to spare us, and raging fires, which certainly won't—and the Mongauli garrison is sure to be wiped out by now, which means—"

"Guin, look out!"

Guin deftly knocked aside an arrow that came flying up the corridor. "Into the room!" he shouted. Swiftly he pushed the three children ahead of him into the narrow chamber, then slammed the stone door shut.

He locked it firmly behind them. "That should hold them for a while—not that we're much better off in here than out there." Outside, the wildlings rained curses on the door, furious at having missed their quarry by mere seconds.

"At least now we're together," said Rinda. "Even if we're to die here, it's better than being apart." She and Remus embraced again, but the little wildling girl Suni scampered over to the corner where she curled into a shivering ball.

"Now, come here Suni," Rinda called gently. "Poor Suni, if they had been from your tribe you'd be safe by now, wouldn't you. Come here, come..."

Suni hesitantly sidled over to the larger girl and clung to her arm.

Guin, watching them, said gruffly, "I will not die here." He paced around the small stone chamber. "I do not even know who I am, or how I came to look like this, and no Nospherus monkey is going to stop me from getting my answers."

"But..."

"Guin!" shouted Remus suddenly. "The door! They're breaking down the door!"

From the other side of the door came a horrendous crash as something very heavy slammed into it. Another crash followed, and another and another until the four in the room could hardly hear themselves think.

"A ram!" Guin laughed. "Those monkeys are smarter than I thought!"

"Guin!" Rinda held her hands together and raised them over her head toward the ceiling. "The Nospherus barbarians take their captives and offer them to their gods—they torture them, and eat them alive, I've heard! If they should break through that door, Guin, I beg you—take your sword and kill us first...and Suni, too, if she wishes it!"

"Rinda!" Remus sobbed, grabbing onto her.

Then they looked up. Over the increasingly deafening crashing of the ram, they could hear Guin laughing.

"The accursed Black Count had it right! You were born with a queen's pride, Rinda Farseer. But you're a little quick to give up. We still have a chance... We must hope until all hope is lost, until our very last breath; we must hope—and fight! That is the true meaning of pride."

Rinda started to protest, but just then the stone door cracked, jagged fissures radiating from a small hole that had opened in its center. Dust and small fragments showered the room. Guin picked up his sword.

"Guin, give me a sword! I'll fight, too," Rinda shouted.

"Get your backs against the wall so they can't surround

you," was Guin's reply. Pushing the three children behind him, he began backing toward the wall farthest from the door, which was concealed behind a thick-woven tapestry.

With a wild cry of victory, the wildlings came leaping through the breached door, waving their stone axes above their heads. Guin found himself fighting for his life once again, but this time the roof was close above him and the room was dark, putting him at a disadvantage. Each time he swung his massive sword, it would hit a wall or skip off the ceiling after taking a Sem's head.

Guin growled and kept retreating.

"We can't go back any further, Guin!" shouted Remus, "we're right up against the—whaaat?" Remus put his hand through the tapestry and toppled. The wall behind had entirely disappeared!

"Ahh!" Rinda's scream trailed off as she, Guin, and Suni followed Remus, sucked into the darkness that opened behind them. An instant later the secret portal that had opened swung back shut, leaving the startled Sem staring at the gently swaying tapestry, a solid stone wall, and nothing else.

—— 3 ——

On the other side of the stone wall yawned endless darkness. The four had fallen, screaming and shouting in surprise at the sudden change in their circumstances, into a hole of unfathomable depth, a blackness that confused their very senses. They had plummeted only for a short distance before they found themselves falling more slowly, almost floating, drifting…until whatever was keeping them suspended dumped them unceremoniously onto a floor of solid stone.

It was their good fortune that Guin, the heaviest of the four, struck the ground first. His trained muscles instinctively took the brunt of the impact, and he caught the three children as they fell on top of him.

The shock of the landing stunned them all, and they lay crumpled on the floor for a short while until Guin stirred, coughed, and began pushing what seemed in the utter darkness to be three little girls off his chest. Soon all four were conscious.

"Everyone okay?" were the first words Guin spoke. His deep growling voice curiously resonated in the darkness.

"I...I'm okay. Rinda?"

"Here...I'm okay too."

The twins found each other with their hands and embraced.

"Why, it's so dark I feel as if I've gone blind! Whatever happened to us? One moment we were in that tower room, and then—"

"Quiet!" rasped Guin in a loud whisper. His eyes burned emerald, visible even in the dark, scanning for any enemy in the pit.

"We fell through the wall in that tower room. It must have been a secret door of some kind leading to this hole...not uncommon in an old castle such as this. Yet whether we are safer now than before, I cannot say."

"I don't like this place," said Rinda, her voice shaking. "There's something unpleasant in this gloom. And the decay I've sensed in this keep from the start—it's here, too. I feel like we're closer to it now than ever before."

"You are the only seer among us, Rinda, and you're right as always," said Guin. "But I didn't need you to warn me of decay. I can feel it myself. It's the stench of flesh that rots even as it lives—worse than the smell of death, it is, and it's been filling my nostrils since we fell down here."

"The Black Count Vanon," whispered Rinda. Then she clapped her hands together. "That's it! Suni and I saw an apparition when we were up in that room—the Black Count. He must have come up through this secret passage and the door behind the tapestry. That's how he disappeared so quickly!"

Speaking hurriedly, Rinda related to Guin and Remus how the monster had come at them, decaying flesh dripping from between its bandages, only disappearing at the last moment before it touched them. She stopped and shivered. "That means he used this passageway. What if his disease is still here, in the air?"

Guin gave a thoughtful growl. His nose wrinkled and his body tightened, and all his instincts screamed *flee!*—but he held himself back.

"There's one thing that doesn't make sense," he said. "How did the count reach the room from this hole? A ladder of some sort? Or perhaps there are steps carved into the wall? Vanon had enough trouble walking; it's hard to imagine him climbing all the way up to that tower. Does this not seem strange?"

"Hmmm..." said Rinda. "There's something else I don't understand. When that thing was attacking Suni and me, it came so close to us, yet when it disappeared, we were unharmed. No skin melting off our bones, no disease." She shivered, remembering the horror in the tower room. "The rotting plague didn't seem to touch us at all—but the Black Count said that if his skin were to so much as touch the air, the plague would infect everyone around him as quick as could be."

"Interesting."

"There is something here in Stafolos Keep," whispered Rinda quietly, as though she were afraid of being overheard by some enemy lurking in the darkness. "It's a mystery, but I am certain that even if the Sem had not attacked tonight, the keep would have fallen before long."

"Well, Rinda Farseer," said Guin, "your prediction matches that of the man that escaped from the room next to ours in the tower: Spellsword, so known for his awareness, much like yours, of danger to come. A mercenary named Istavan, he—what's wrong, child?"

Guin had been chuckling as he talked, but he stopped when he felt a jolt where Rinda's body touched his own; it was as if a bolt of lightning had shot through her as he spoke the mercenary's name.

"You know this Istavan...of Valachia, was it? The 'Crimson Mercenary'?"

Rinda stuttered. "I...no, I don't, but..." She reached out and wrapped her hands around Guin's powerful arm. A shiver ran through her, as if she had heard the little fate-wheel of Jarn's loom turn, and she remembered having a similar feeling the moment she had first called the leopard-headed warrior by his name. The sound of the mercenary's name, "Istavan"—although she was sure she had never heard it before—caused her stomach to tighten and her hands to shake. She, who was blessed by the gods with a power to see things that could not be seen, grabbed on tighter to Guin's arm. Just touching his powerful body she could feel his strength lapping over her like the tide, and she felt braver and more at ease.

"What is it, Rinda?...you *see* something, don't you?" Remus asked, peeved at being left out of the conversation. He loved his sister well, but he couldn't help feeling pangs of jealousy whenever she showed signs of that power he did not have. He felt that he had been singled out, left behind holding the short straw.

"I don't know...it's just my nerves, I'm sure," she replied, squirming in closer between Guin and her brother. "Isn't it about time we stopped sitting around in the dark, anyway?"

"If indeed there is a way out of here," Guin muttered glumly, slowly lifting himself off the ground to begin searching in the total blackness. He couldn't even see his hand lifted before his face.

Suddenly, the little Sem girl Suni, quiet up until now, began chattering in her high-pitched tongue. When Guin replied in kind, it gave the twins quite a start.

"Guin! You—you know her language, I mean, you can speak it!"

"Just who are you, Guin?"

"Quiet, this is important," he snapped, then explained: "She can see in the dark, she says; all her kind can; and because she knows we are her friends, she will help us find a way out." He began speaking as she chattered, providing a running translation. "The pit we are in isn't that big, and there's something set into the wall, a lift of some sort. And...there's a wall, a dead end only fifty paces from where we're sitting. She's going to check to see if it's another secret door."

"But we don't know what might be on the other side! Don't go, Suni!"

"We cannot remain sitting here for all eternity. It is a risk we have to take," Guin declared with finality. "Do not worry. Whatever may lie beyond that wall, I luckily did not lose my sword in the fall, and I am not afraid to take another life."

"What if what's behind that wall is already dead, Guin?" said Rinda, a hint of anger in her voice. "What if that walking corpse is out—" she stopped, hearing a chirp from a short distance away in the dark.

"Suni! Suni?!"

Remus had to hold onto his sister to keep her from running out blindly into the dark.

"She says there's a door there," explained Guin, grabbing the twins by the shoulders. "We go!"

"But the Black Count—" began Remus, stopping short when he heard Suni shriek and then, just as abruptly, go silent.

A narrow light sliced through the darkness, and Guin charged towards it, dragging the twins along behind him.

"The door spun...and Suni's on the other side!" he growled.

"Suni! Suni!" Rinda ran up and began pounding on the wall with her small fists, forgetting entirely her fear that the very halls where the Black Count lurked might lie on the other side.

As it happened, she chanced to hit just the spot that Suni had found, triggering the mechanism that sent the whole wall spinning. The secret portal whipped the three companions around and spit them out on the other side, immediately closing tight behind them.

The three tumbled out onto the stone floor, their senses reeling at the sudden change in their surroundings. Compared to the blind darkness in which they had been, the place where they found themselves now was brilliant, and it took a while for their eyes to adjust—whereupon they perceived an underground chamber with a low ceiling, much like many others they had seen in the keep, that wasn't very brightly lit after all. In fact, it was positively gloomy.

On closer inspection, the damp, narrow room seemed to be part of a longer hall with pillars that ran along each side. There was no one about, no Sem—not even the little girl Suni who surely had come through the door before them. The only sound was the sound of water dripping down the stone walls.

"I know this place," said Guin, looking around. "We are underneath the black tower, where I was brought before." He raised his longsword and warily stepped out into the hall, waving for the twins to follow after confirming that no danger was near.

"Yes, they took me through here. This hall leads to the count's torture room."

"So there is a secret passage connecting the white tower to the black," said Rinda softly. "That's how the count was able to pay his visits to the captives—the sacrifices—that his underlings put in the white."

"So it seems."

Guin continued scanning back and forth, checking for lurking dangers in the shadows behind the pillars before he advanced with the children close beside him.

"I wonder what happened to Suni?"

"Who knows? Gone on ahead, perhaps; hopefully she escaped whatever frightened her."

"She wouldn't just leave us here like that—she's so small and fearful."

Rinda looked carefully down both sides of the corridor. Nothing was stirring in the dim light that pooled behind the long rows of pillars along the rough-hewn stone walls. So complete was the stillness, it was hard to believe that the keep above was swarming with the victorious Sem invaders. Down here, there was only an oppressive silence and solitude that tempted Rinda to think nothing that had happened in the last few hours was real at all. Only the faint, cloying stench of decay seeping from an unknown source served to remind her whose halls these were, and to keep her wits on edge.

"Suni! Suni!" Rinda's call echoed down the stone corridor.

"Quiet. We don't know what's listening." Guin's reprimand silenced her. "I walked this very hall but several hours ago—to the right, here, it goes upward to the keep-lord's torture chamber. I remember seeing prisoners there." Guin thought, then spoke again: "If we free them, and they are willing to fight, we might just have a chance against the Sem."

"But, Suni!"

"Suni is a Sem. She will not need our help to evade her own kind."

Guin kept the children safe behind him as they approached the entrance to the large hall where the black knights had brought him on the way to fight the grey ape.

"Stay here."

Guin held his sword ready, and moved soundlessly up into the area where he had seen the count's torturing platforms lying side by side.

"What?!" the leopard-man nearly shouted in his surprise. Remus and Rinda quickly stepped out into the hall behind him.

"No one! No slaves, no prisoners, not even that accursed count!"

"Maybe the Sem got them?"

"No..." Guin scanned the chamber, baffled. "Wildlings leave corpses, blood, traces of battle. The only thing left of the prisoners here is their chains."

It was a strangely chilling sight. In the middle of the large, dim chamber, an assortment of torturing devices made a gloomy procession, arranged in a crooked line as twisted as the mind of the keep-lord who used them. The horrible machines had been disturbing enough when slaves with the eyes of corpses stood by to work them; but seeing them now, unmoving, their chains and empty shackles hanging crookedly from the stone platforms and wicked iron mechanisms, was somehow far more ghastly.

"What could have happened here?" Guin said in a sunken voice. "Nothing makes sense. How can it be that there is no living person, slave or otherwise, in the black tower? Where did they all go?"

"Guin, I'm scared." Remus hugged himself tightly and moved nearer to the others.

"Me too," Rinda admitted. A mob of attacking Sem, or the Black Count himself in all his pestilence, might mean certain

death, but at least such threats would have given the companions something to fight. In this kind of absolute silence, devoid
of life, where not even the air moved, the only thing left to
resist was dark, oppressive fear...

"Guin! We must leave this place!" Rinda's voice was high
and wavering. "Nothing good is here. I'd rather have death by
the hands of the Sem than this. Let's go back."

"No," Guin replied, firmly shaking his head. His leopard
eyes shone. "Going back is certain death. Be this place accursed
and vile, at least this way there is hope. Do not fear, children.
Should the count's rotting disease fall upon your flesh and
infect you, I will be swift to give you rest with my sword."

"Promise me! Do you swear?"

"By this damned leopard head, I swear it." Guin lifted his
sword. "Through that corridor is the arena where I fought the
grey ape—and I saw another, darker passage leading from its far
side. If my instincts serve me well, beyond that are stairs into
the black tower...or at least a passage leading somewhere."

The three friends kept close together, their hearts racing
every time they heard the sound of water dripping from the
walls. Slowly they made their way across the lifeless chamber.

"Look there," Guin told them as they entered another
empty chamber. "There, where the floor is lower, is where I
killed the grey ape. You can see the iron cage in which they kept

the beast further back. It still smells of ape, and as my muscles ache I know it was no dream...but where is the body?"

"They must have cleaned it up," Remus ventured.

"Or maybe they had another way to get rid of the body." Guin chuckled darkly.

The twins clung tightly to either side of the warrior, like two tiny white rock-lilies clinging to the sides of a massive boulder. The only sound in the room was their echoing footsteps; they made their way to the exit at the far side without meeting any resistance, living or otherwise.

"Our real trial lies beyond," said Guin in a low voice, putting the twins behind him again.

As he had guessed, a thin stair rose beyond the arched entrance. It went twisting up through the gloom until it disappeared around a corner. The place seemed oddly familiar; after a moment they realized that this stair was nearly identical to the one in the white tower.

Guin hesitated before stepping through the archway—a show of caution unusual for the bold leopard warrior. He felt a curious shiver running through his body. All his senses were screaming that there was something waiting up there in the clammy darkness.

"Do you feel something in there, Rinda?" he asked, partly to conceal his unease, gesturing through the gloom at the stairs that led up between narrow walls ahead of them. And Rinda, holding on to her brother, closed her eyes and *saw*. She whispered back to the leopard-man as though she were afraid of the darkness itself hearing her.

"The most evil thing is in there, Guin. Yet so, too, is our path to freedom."

"Then it seems we must confront whatever thing it is that makes its nest in this keep. There is no avoiding it," he said, fearlessly stepping forward. A grim light flamed in his yellowish eyes. It occurred to Remus that the burning light was like a signal: Guin, the man inside the mask, had gone to sleep, and the soul of the leopard whose face he wore now possessed him entirely.

"Follow close, children," Guin told them, walking warily but without hesitation towards the stair. Once again, the tepid darkness drew near and enveloped him, as though it had a living will of its own, an insatiable hunger. The twins followed him into it.

They climbed a length of stair, turned a corner, and climbed again. Rinda bit her lip to keep from crying aloud; she could feel her brother's warm fingers holding her arm, lending her strength, but it was not enough. To him, this place might be scary or unnerving, but to her, as sensitive to the spirit world as she was, it shrieked of danger—in the feel of the viscous darkness on her skin, in the wafting stench of rot that filled her nostrils, she felt the presence that watched over the whole tower, everywhere and yet nowhere. This was Doal's domain, and she wanted no part of it.

The stairs turned and twisted, until Rinda wasn't sure whether they were actually climbing, or whether they were just endlessly going around the same corner, treading the same steps over and over.

Then they heard it: a faint, muffled sob, as if someone was crying through a cloth gag. It was high-pitched, like that of a little girl, but the timbre had a distinct quality that suggested its owner was not quite human.

"Suni!" shouted Rinda.

Guin dashed forward, following his keen sense of hearing toward the faint voice—one more floor up, and then to the right. He took the last few steps in a single stride, stopping at the head of a dark corridor that seemed to branch off into many rooms. The smell of decay was nearly unbearable.

The warrior lifted his sword and abruptly kicked in the nearest door—and gasped. There, in a stone-walled room much like those in the white tower, was a mountain of bones, gleaming an eerie white in the dim light.

"Oh!" the twins gasped in unison.

"Wrong door," shouted Guin, running to the next door, and the next.

There, he wavered, and stepped back. His foot had swung

to kick the door and met with nothing but empty space—the door had opened by itself, becoming a fissure that looked in at...nothing—a dark emptiness like the void of space itself, except that it stank of death.

From somewhere within that darkness they could hear Suni, bound and crying; but then—

The three involuntarily stepped back.

Framed by the stone doorway, an armored figure emerged from the reeking void.

Its faceplate was lowered, a black mask drawn over face and nose, the metal of its armor clanging and creaking as it waveringly advanced: an ancient apparition compounded of every nightmare that ever had been. Its movements were unnatural, slow and stiff; it was like a massive caricature, a martial marionette, powered by terror and black magic.

Rinda screamed, a weak scream that caught halfway along her throat, coming out in choked bits and pieces.

"The...Black...Count...!"

There was something about the wavering armored warrior surrounded by endless darkness that profaned all providence— a denial of the very spark of life, a horror that spread from its form and covered everything in filth. The figure threw its head back, and laughed.

Then the keep-lord of Stafolos spoke.

—— 4 ——

"Leopard-man." The Black Count's voice made a hollow, rustling noise, like a winter wind blowing through the skeletal branches of a withered tree. "You did well to get past the Sem and come all the way here, bringing the twins of Parros without a scratch! For this, in particular, I must thank you."

Guin did not answer. Shielding the twins with his body, he glared at the count. His eyes flamed, the fangs in his rigid jaw gleamed with a sudden white brilliance, and he held his sword poised to strike.

"I was worried, you see," rasped the count. "I sent my black knights to fetch the twins from the white tower, but those filthy monkeys had already taken the keep proper and were in the tower by the time my knights arrived. You—all three of you—are too valuable to risk losing to those barbarians: a warrior worth his weight in gold in the arena, and the Pearls of Parros, keepers of its secrets—no?"

Rinda shouted. "Let Suni go! The Sem will be here any moment! She can parley with them for peace!" The figure looming before her was too frightful for words, yet seeing Suni tied up behind him on some horrible device, struggling and crying when she saw them come into the room, filled Rinda's heart with an indignant wrath so strong it overcame her fear.

"My young princess of Parros, do you know what this device is for?" asked the count with a rasping, derisive laugh. "There is only one drug that eases the symptoms of my disease, the black plague I carry—I must squeeze it from the living, down to the last drop."

Rinda railed at him, calling him a vampire and worse, yet he continued on as though she did not even exist. "It is my daily nourishment—yet only the freshest blood suffices. Then I slice off slivers of flesh from the drained body and press them to my skin—it slows the plague's advance..."

Rinda was furious. "How many innocent Sem have you killed? It was Janos himself who cast the flames on Stafolos Keep! This is your punishment, monster!"

"If this keep must fall, then so be it," the count replied coldly. "It is all set in Jarn's weave, is it not? If that divine bastard had even a drop of pity in him, would he have let me live thus? Jarn has set our fate, and Janos has nodded his approval, so who am I, who curse at them rather than pray to them, to say what should happen to Stafolos? In fact, why not accept that my

existence is a curse, and spread my disease all over my homeland of Mongaul—yes, throw my plague right in the very face of
its master Janos, and the dotard Jarn and his damned loom! I'll
smear my filth all over their world."

"Count Vanon!" thundered Guin, whose eyes, flaming
yellow, had been silently watching the lord of Stafolos Keep
rant against the gods. "Your curses would make Doal proud,
I'm sure, but there is one thing you forget."

"And what is that, beast-man?" said the count, stiffly raising his hand. "Whatever you say, keep in mind that I could peel
off my armor at any time and change you and the twins of
Parros to rotting lumps of flesh."

"Go ahead," said Guin, calmly stepping forward.

Rinda screamed. "Guin! Stay away from that thing!"

Guin stepped forward again, and again, moving closer.

"I'll spread my plague! I'll do it!" the Black Count
screeched. "Don't come any closer, half-man! I'll rip the mask
off my face and visit a destruction upon this keep so total that
the Sem and the flames will seem a child's prank in compari-
son!" His hand slid up to the fastenings on his chest plate. The
children screamed for Guin to stop, yet he strode forward still,
holding up his longsword.

"You...You do not fear the black plague, leopard?!"

"I do fear it," replied Guin, "but I said you were forgetting something: you are not the Black Count of Mongaul!"

Suddenly, Guin swung his longsword down through the helm and armor that wrapped around the count's body, cutting him in two halves from head to toe!

Rinda and Remus screamed in unison, but the sound of their voices was drowned out by an even louder death wail that sliced through the air around them. The twins screamed again, and drew back, looking with unbelieving eyes at what was left of the count.

No sloughing, melting flesh, no fallen wreck of a man, no spreading plague of pestilence and death.

"Guin! There...there's nothing there!"

"This is the true form of the evil that lurks in Stafolos Keep—this is your 'Black Count'!" shouted Guin, leaping over the split suit of armor to pull the little Sem girl from the evil-looking contraption on the wall. "It is nothing but a haunt, an evil spirit. No count—and no black plague!"

But it was untrue to say that there was nothing in the suit of armor at all, for now a black, swirling *something* was coalescing on the floor in front of the twins as they held hands trembling. It was like a darkness born of greater darkness, a living, black mist slowly gathering itself into a writhing, monstrous presence. It was an animate emptiness, a moving void—yet clearly it had a will, it was very much alive, and it possessed the intelligence that had enabled it to impersonate the count for a very long time. Rinda felt the bile rise in her throat. Her trembling, white fingers hurriedly made the sign of Janos to ward off curses and spirits. But she stopped halfway through, her hands frozen in place.

"Guin! It's coming this way!"

Guin whirled around. The darkness that rose from the broken armor shell was growing physically palpable, the wisps joining together to form a vaguely human shape. The sight was nauseating.

Through the translucent mass, Guin could see the twins huddling together. Grabbing Suni by her hairy arm, he charged towards the thing, slashing through it three times with his sword.

"No, Guin, stop!" Rinda screamed.

The entity wobbled, seeming to split apart with the blows, but then it slid back together, its shape even more clearly defined now, and its hellish desire even more plain. It advanced on the twins, sensing warm, living blood.

"Run!" Guin shouted to the twins. "It's a wraith—akin to the ghouls in the Roodwood! This is what left those bones we found! Run, quickly!"

The twin Pearls of Parros had already started back up the corridor, fleeing toward the stairs. Guin brought up the rear, slashing at the spirit whenever it drew close and retreating when he could. His sword was but a poor weapon against the thing—all he could do was slow the creature down—but at least he was buying them time. As he furiously swung his sword, trying to keep the thing from reforming, he shouted back to the children: "Don't go up, or we'll be trapped! We leave through the corridor below!"

"Guin!" Remus was just about to step onto the stairs when he called back. "We can't go this way, Guin! The Sem are in the tower!"

"The Sem are breaking through the door below! I can hear them!" shouted Rinda.

"Wildlings from below, and a wraith from behind!" roared Guin. "It seems Jarn in his kindness has seen fit to give us a taste of every predicament there is! Fine—we go up!"

The twins shouted their agreement, but instead of heading up the stairs, they waited for him to catch up. The sound of a ram hitting the door far below rang louder, accompanied by the high-pitched victory cries of the Sem. Now and then, the companions heard a human voice—one of the few remaining knights shouting desperate orders to protect the tower, or the keep-lord—but they never heard a reply other than the sound of swords clanging on stone.

"They give their lives to protect this fiend?" spat Guin.

Then, hearing the door below give way at last, he abandoned his futile battle and ran to the children, urging them up the stairs. "We can outrun the wraith at least," he shouted, nearly out of breath, "and if those Sem come up as quickly as I think, they will—"

A great commotion broke out below them on the stair. The wraith had found a source of living flesh more immediate than Guin and the children—it was like a ravenous bear wandering into a pack of feral dogs. The wildlings gave a tremendous battle cry and charged, not even giving the wraith time to choose which it would feast on first.

"Now's our chance! Run!" Guin barked. Yet they had only climbed four floors higher when they came to a dead end: a heavy stone door stood between them and the single small room, like that in the white tower, at which the long stair terminated.

"Not again!" the leopard-man growled furiously.

"What was that thing?" Remus asked. "If it was only pretending to be the Black Count Vanon, then what happened to the real count?"

"If I'm not mistaken, the real count was the first one it ate," Guin replied. "Perhaps he was searching in the Marches for answers to his own disease, and brought back someone the wraith had possessed. Once the thing consumed the count, it could order victims brought to it and eat them at its leisure. I assume the fiend also took on some of the count's knowledge, so it had no problem impersonating the keep-lord, especially as Vanon was so reclusive. A surprising show of intelligence for a mere Roodwood spirit..."

"So then, the real Count Vanon..."

Before Guin had finished saying "turned into a pile of white bones some time ago," Rinda cried, pointing ahead of them. Guin turned to look, and froze.

Somehow, without a sound, an apparition had appeared beyond them in the dead end of the gloomy stone corridor. It looked even wispier than the wraith; its silhouette was vague, little more than a faint shadow on the wall, nor had it the presence of the living darkness they could hear fighting the Sem below.

Yet it did have a form, just enough to distinguish the tall stature of a nobleman, covered in hastily wrapped bandages and shadowed in a deep-hooded cloak. The skin that was visible through the wrappings on its face and body was black and sagging, a grim gruel of rotting flesh split open in places to show the white gleam of bone beneath.

But what was far more terrible than the sagging flesh of its body, and far more piteous, were the eyes that shone with a wet gleam from a break in the bandages that covered its mostly hairless head. They were white and clouded, and almost certainly could no longer see, yet they were unmistakably human, clinging to some almost-forgotten memory of the intellect and consciousness they had once possessed.

Rinda shivered. Surely this was the same accursed apparition that had visited her in the white tower.

"Count Vanon..."

"Yes," whispered Guin, averting his gaze, "the real count was eaten long ago, but his death was cursed and he was not allowed to enter the underworld, so he roams the keep in the form he had during life...watching that imposter destroy whatever vestiges of pride he had left."

"Poor Vanon..." Rinda murmured, genuine pity welling in her heart. "What a horrid fate...to have your body eaten by a Roodwood ghoul, yet still to be cursed with the same miserable form in death as you had in life."

"At least, this way, he was able to spare his homeland from the ravages of the disease he carried," said Guin, extending his left hand toward the apparition and making a strange sign, like a ward, in the air.

"Black Count!

"The Sem have taken Stafolos Keep, or soon will, and the blaze will have it if they do not. The Roodwood wraith will have to abandon its charade, and the fires will purge it in the end.

Fire will purify all. Your disease, the wraith's foul work—all will be purged in the fire that takes Stafolos Keep.

"Now, go to your rest in the underworld! Your master Doal awaits you, apparition!"

Guin's voice rang clear in the stone corridor.

The ghost slowly raised its hands, seeming to make a gesture—with its indeterminate form, it was impossible to divine just what. Still, Rinda thought she could see something that looked like peace in those clouded eyes.

It was then that Rinda realized. When this same apparition had appeared before her and Suni in the tower room, it had reached out to them, she had thought, to attack. But that strange pathos, the longing in its eyes, was a plea for salvation. It had been trying to tell them of the fate that had befallen the keep; it had been in pain. Tears welled in her eyes.

"What could he have possibly done that Janos would punish him so?" said the girl, shaking her head. "I cannot think of anything that would warrant it."

"It is because your soul still sleeps in the cradle of youth, little princess. I can think of a few things he might have done," said Guin, but the bleak jest in his voice faded as he listened at the stairway. "Wait, they are coming!" he shouted. "The Sem are coming up the stairs!"

The constant sounds of battle below them were suddenly

much closer. The wraith had claimed many of the wildlings, but even that had not slowed them. Meanwhile, the monster had grown with each kill, until their axes and arrows could do little to harm it—and what real harm could stone blade and poisoned shaft do to something made of nothing but the darkness itself?

Guin readied his longsword. Dried blood turning black caked his blade and the arms that held it, made brighter by more blood that had sprayed on top of that. He could keep fighting, yes, but soon a stone axe or a swift Sem arrow was bound to break through his guard and catch one of his legs, already weak with exhaustion, and then surely he would die there in that dead-end corridor at the tower's top. There was only one way out, and that was down. All he could do here was wait for death to come, whether it was from the great army of the Sem, the voracious wraith, or the smoke and flames of the fire that crackled and grew among the buildings of the keep.

Guin howled and raised his sword, taking a few swings to limber up his stiffened arms.

But Rinda grabbed on to his elbow to get his attention.

"Look!"

Guin turned around. The apparition was moving away from them, slowly fading. As it moved, it was making exaggerated gestures with its arm, pointing up at the stone ceiling above them. Again and again, it pointed at a particular spot on the ceiling. A light that seemed to come from the very depths of space shone in its eyes...until the ghost of the diseased lord reached the far wall and vanished into it—the Black Count Vanon, gone at last.

"The ceiling! There must be something there!"

"Let's hope it's a way out," Guin growled, reaching out toward the ceiling where the count's apparition had pointed.

For a while it seemed like another section of featureless stone, but then the leopard warrior's sword caught on some sort of hidden lever, and a trap door popped open in the ceiling, letting in a fresh evening breeze and light from the faded sky of the lingering day.

The twins and Suni cheered.

"Climb!" said Guin, lifting Rinda up toward the small square hole. When she had adroitly scrambled through, he lifted the other two up after her. Just then the Sem broke past the wraith, arriving at the top floor of the tower in strength. Brandishing their weapons, they filled the narrow space with their piercing war cries.

Guin snarled and swung his blade, cutting down the first wildlings as they swarmed toward him.

"Guin! Quickly! Are you okay?" came the nervous shouts of the twins from above.

"Get away from the opening, now!" Guin shouted back, his sword flying furiously as he single-handedly took on the full brunt of the wildling attack. There seemed to be no end to them—and from the ever-nearing cacophony behind them, it sounded like the wraith was also coming up the stairs, slaughtering Sem as it came. Guin laid low the two nearest of his foes, sending up a crimson spray, and then turned his back on the rest and leapt for the hole in the ceiling.

His powerful hands grabbed on to the edge of the opening and he lifted himself up with a fluidity of motion uncanny for his size, kicking off the Sem that clung to his legs and waist. His wide shoulders caught on the sides of the hole for a moment, but he twisted and slid through on the diagonal. He was free! Guin stood and breathed a deep sigh of relief.

They were on top of the black tower. The day that had begun in battle was trying to end before the battle was over. Looking down on the buildings of the keep below, they saw the courtyards and parapets buried in bodies. Inky black smoke rose on all sides, signaling the fall of the keep to the world.

They could also see the dark, deep flow of the Kes below, the slanting dusk light glinting off its surface. And there was the Roodwood, the Taloswood, the mystic dusky-violet mountains in the distance…and the wildlands of Nospherus stretching beyond the black river.

The sun was starting to set, a giant, dusky orange half-sphere throwing its last reddish rays on the ruined fortress. Guin stood with the sun at his back, his sword in his hand.

Rinda, Remus, and the little girl Suni held their breath as they looked at the warrior with the body of a hero and the head of a leopard, standing tall with the giant corona of the sun's red disk behind him, a bloodied sword in his hand. He could have been a statue to the half-beast god Cirenos, or even the war god Ruah—horrible, yet at the same time a thing of beauty. The ruddy light spread over his smooth, rippling muscles like a baptism of blood. He was poised with one foot upon the flag stand that marked the very top of the tower, holding on to the flagpole with his free hand.

"Guin!"

He reacted in a flash to Rinda's warning, leaping down to where the first of the wildlings was climbing up through the opening in the roof. With a flick of his sword, he sent its head flying off the tower to land in the courtyard far below. He kicked the next attacker back down into the corridor, and shouted, "There is no end to this if we stay here! Children! I am going, will you follow?"

"Wh-Where, Guin? We're on the top of the tower! Where is there to go from here?"

"There!" howled Guin, pointing down to one side.

The children gasped. Down where he pointed was only the deep, silent flow of the Kes.

"If we jump, we may die. The sun is about to set: we will face the Marches night in those dark waters. We may be knocked out and slip under. But know this—staying here is certain death."

"I understand," said Rinda. "I will go."

"Me...Me too," said Remus, suppressing his fear.

"Good," Guin replied. Moving quickly, he loosened his belt and used it to fasten the three children onto his back. The wildlings trying to stream up through the opening were already too many for him to handle alone.

"Close your eyes, keep your heads down, and hold on!" shouted the leopard warrior, and like a bird, he leapt off into space.

Towards freedom—and destiny.

END OF BOOK ONE

Coming in January 2008

THE GUIN SAGA, BOOK TWO: Warrior in the Wilderness

by KAORU KURIMOTO

Paperback
288 pages
5.5 x 7.5 inches
$9.95/$12.95

The Archduke Vlad's own daughter, General Amnelis, leads an expeditionary force to punish the Sem! She also wishes to investigate reports that the Pearls of Parros have been seen in the Marches. Standing between them—Guin!

Get Volume One Now!

THE GUIN SAGA *Manga*
The Seven Magi

ILLUSTRATED BY
KAZUAKI YANAGISAWA
STORY BY
KAORU KURIMOTO

Paperback, 172 pages
6 x 8 inches, $12.95/$17.95

Many years after awaking in the Roodwood, the leopard-headed warrior has become King of Cheironia. Only he can dispel the black plague that ravishes his realm.
A three-volume manga based on the first *gaiden* side story of the saga. Ages 16 and up.